New Hall

New Hall

Kathy James

DEDICATION

The author will donate money received from the sale of this book to Rethink Mental Illness: a registered charity offering support to those experiencing severe mental illness, their carers and relatives.

.

ACKNOWLEDGEMENTS

This book would not have been possible without the help
and guidance of Sylvia Croxall.

Cover design by Michael Trim
.

THE STORM

Storm-force waves broke over the prow and pummelled the sides of the Southern Star. The sound of terrified horses came from below, their unearthly squeals cutting through the rush of wind and sea. Scowling at the skies, the Captain turned querulously to his Deck Officer: "Where the devil's that gipsy fellow?"

"I believe he went below at the first sign of the squall, Sir."

"If he can handle horses as they say, now's the time to do it. Go and see what he's about."

On first going below-decks, the Officer could not see the horse-handler but, as his eyes grew used to the poor light, he spotted him leaning forward along the neck of the black stallion; his hand resting between the flaring nostrils and his mouth tight up against the horse's ears. The Spanish stallion stood stock still but the signs of his terror were seen in the panting of his sides and the trampled bedding. Tied to the side of the ship with twine, the stallion had broken free and found his own sea legs when a stronger restraint would have harmed him.

As the stallion grew calm, the mares' screams changed to whinnies and the handler turned his attention to them all. With plangent tones, his voice reached out to them in a strange lilting language that cut through the churning of the seas. Without raising his voice, he drew the horses to him: the mares nudging against each other, as if nodding in agreement. A grey mare, already heavy with foal, turned to face the ship's Officer and breathed out a slow, deep-throated sigh. She was wary but content.

The Officer neither moved nor tried to address the handler. Despite the gipsy's lowly status, the horse stalls were his absolute domain: he had sole responsibility and also sole authority. Turning on his heel, the Deck Officer returned to report that all was well.

NEW HALL

The storm at sea had also brought damage to the south coast of England. A diseased elm had fallen and flying debris had smashed a row of glass frames in the kitchen- garden at New Hall. John Graves, the Estates manager, was receiving reports from the head gardener when the Duke of Shire came on a tour of inspection.

"Much damage, Mr Graves?" he asked, looking across the Great Park toward the gatehouse.

"We escaped the worst of it, your Grace, and we'll have the tree cleared away by lunch time."

"Good man! The horses arrive later and I want everything to go smoothly. They had a hard time of it, at sea, if they faced the same winds that claimed the old elm."

The Duke turned back to the house. Slightly stooped but an impressive figure for a man in his seventies, he still rode to hounds and rarely failed to make his daily rounds of the gardens. The house had been in the Wellesden family since the seventeenth century when "New Hall" had replaced the moated manor house that pre-dated it. The old Duke was scorned by some for his lack of style but his hands-on approach to the Estate had kept his inheritance intact at a time when others were glamorously and dramatically losing theirs. However, his heir, the Marquess of Wellesden, had other interests. With widespread investments elsewhere, he used the income from New Hall to keep his son, Harry, "in with the right set"; and out of trouble.

******

Marianne Graves ran up the steps to the terrace. Her father was studying the clouds and frowning at the prospect of further rain. She touched his elbow gently and John's face broke into a delighted smile. He turned and kissed her forehead with studied formality, however. Marianne had none of her father's British diffidence. Her vitality came solely from her French mother: as did the chestnut hair and black-brown eyes.

"Papa," she began with a mock-serious expression. "You promised I could come with you and yet here you are and I've spent half an hour looking for you."

Her English was unaccented and clear; only the "Papa" betrayed her mother's native tongue. As a child, French had been the language of lullaby and endearment. When Marianne's mother died in a riding accident, just before her daughter's twelfth birthday, Marianne continued to go to France every summer, at the insistence of Tante Jeanne. Her mother's spinster sister, Tante Jeanne had presided over her niece's musical education as well as encouraging her love of French.

Father and daughter turned the corner of the house, naturally falling into step with one another. The sun was breaking through the cloud. The night's storm had polished the lawns to a glistening green and gave a sense of expectation to the day. Thin trails of smoke came from the crenulated chimneys and the house glowed yellow in the morning light. John looked down at his daughter.

"I missed spending the summers with you, Chouchou"

Marianne smiled at his use of her nickname and adopted a mischievous tone.

"Missed all my tempers and tantrums? Missed me forever asking, why? I'd think you'd be pleased to have Tante Jeanne give you some respite by whisking me away."

"It's true, you were not an easy child," her father replied with an air of understatement.

"But here I am: a 'delightful young woman': transformed by my French Aunts from 'a problem to a pleasure'. These are the very words of Great Aunt Isabelle and while everyone agrees that Tante Jeanne may, on occasion, make allowances; no one could ever say that of Aunt Isabelle. In fact, we all know that there is no greater authority on the subject of proper behaviour in the whole world than Great Aunt Isabelle - so my delightfulness must be beyond question."

Her father laughed out loud at the mock curtsy which she made him and tucked her arm back under his. Looking out across the rain-spangled park he finally managed a gruff: "Your mother would be proud, I know."

Neither spoke as the words hung in the air, so Robert Baker's greeting cut into their shared thoughts and startled the both of them.

"Good morning, Mr Graves, Miss Graves. I hope I find you well?"

Robert removed his hat and steadied the folder that he was carrying under his arm. "I've come with the accounts," he explained. "I'd welcome your comment before I present them."

John held out his hand.

"I'm happy to give them a glance but they are always impeccable. You're better at this kind of thing than I ever was."

Since John had taught Robert most of what he knew about book-keeping, the response was possibly exaggerated but it showed the mutual regard in which they held each other. Though ten years younger than John, Robert now farmed over 100 acres of New Hall land and much of the land owned by John Graves himself. The two men had known each other all their lives and, despite the formality of their working relationship, they were friends and allies.

Sensing that Robert was about to leave, Marianne stepped forward:

"Will you not join us for a cup of tea?" she asked, in her

best grown-up manner.

"That's a very kind offer, but you must forgive me. I've business in Swanton and I need to get the 10 o'clock train."

"Another time, then," replied Marianne, grandly — relishing her role as hostess.

NEW BLOOD

Finally, the long-awaited horses had arrived. The handler rode at the head of a string of horses: bareback, on a "workaday horse". Indeed, his mount had an almost comical look. She was broad in the shoulder and dun-coloured, with a patch over one eye and a streaked mane and tale; more suited to a circus than her present well-bred company. Her solid indifference to her surroundings seemed to have mesmerised the other horses, however, and they followed her, two-by-two, like children on a Sunday school outing. The stallion brought up the rear; occasionally breaking into a skittish side step but keeping his distance and not spooking the others.

As the strange procession approached the house, the Duke was called to the stable yard. Capable hands took charge of the mares as the handler brought the newly-alarmed stallion alongside his mount. The comical horse nuzzled the stallion's shoulder as if they were long-time friends and the stallion whinnied in reply. The Duke ran his experienced eye over all three as John asked the handler to dismount.

"This is His Grace, the Duke of Newton," John said in French, with an English accent broader than a navvy's back.

The handler turned to the Duke and, with the merest suggestion of a bow of the head, he offered him the stallion's rope. The Duke gently reached out to stroke the stallion's neck, running his fingers down the fine-etched muscles. As he did so, the handler watched horse and man, seeming to appraise them both.

"So this is Hidalgo? He's wonderful! Better than I had even imagined! Will you show me his paces?" the Duke asked, addressing the handler in an antique French learned from his tutor some sixty years ago.

The handler took the rope and, with another nod of recognition, walked the stallion round in front of the clock, urging him to a trot at the far end of the yard and halting back in front of His Lordship.

"He's a fine horse and you have done a fine job getting him here. Mr Graves, have one of the stable lads lead the way to Hidalgo's stable and make sure that both horse and man are made comfortable. Le Comte de Gilles offered to have his stableman stay in England until we have introduced Hidalgo to Gloriana. The sooner we can get her in foal, the sooner the bloodline is ensured."

The handler moved forward as the Duke turned to go. Looking His Grace straight in the eye, he drew his hand to his heart and finally bowed his head.

"Fabrice Dupres, à votre service, Milor – Ce cheval magnifique sera bien chez vous. Lui aussi, il a de la noblesse." The Duke returned his gaze and they went their separate ways.

Jem Snapes, the stable lad, was proud of his long legs that made him far taller than most fourteen year olds but he barely managed to scramble alongside the stallion as Fabrice walked him round to the stable. Leaving Jem with the comical mare, Fabrice checked the stall for broken edges and tested the bedding for its depth and quality, lifting the feed to his nose before allowing the stallion to eat. The Head Stableman looked on affronted then pushed his way into the stable.

"You'll not find better, not here nor in France, my lad," he said abruptly to the handler while stepping forward and causing Hidalgo to roll his eyes and flatten his ears.

"You'll best be out of there now. Get your own horse

and be off round the back to your quarters."

The handler looked at him uncomprehendingly but Peter Robinson was determined to show his authority and he placed a hand on the handler's shoulder as a means of propelling him toward the door. Fabrice bridled and rudely shook the hand away. He glared both at Peter Robinson and the lads who had gathered in the yard. With an extra fierce glare at Jem, he looked round for his forsaken horse. "Belle," he shouted. The comic horse appeared, with tell-tale food around her mouth. She sank her head and made to look ashamed - much in the same way as Jem was doing - but to greater effect. Even Peter had to smile and the mood of the group had been lightened as Jem re-captured the wily Belle.

Fabrice went to move toward the doorway but now his way was barred by two newcomers. Young Lord Harry and his visitor, Lord Brandon: the heir to the Duke of Kinshire, had come to look at the acclaimed stallion and the stable lads were making a pathway for them through the crowd. Without knowing how much in agreement they were, both the Head Stableman and Fabrice spoke together: but Peter raised his cap. "My apologies, my Lord, but the stallion has only just settled and he is very highly-strung. It would be better for the horse if you came back later. If you would be so kind, Sir?"

Lord Harry did not waver one inch and his friend the Marquess of Kinshire sniggered.

"He needs to be alone," said the handler, in French. "And you need to get rid of those cigars," he added, moving back into the doorway.

"It seems the gipsy rover has different ideas," exclaimed the Marquess. "Maybe he needs a lesson in manners as well as tuition in the English language."

"Get out of my way," said Lord Harry, waving the cigar very close to Fabrice. "I'll be damned if I'm told when I can enter my own stables."

"Ahh, but he's a French Frog, Wellesden. Son of the revolution and all that. Equality, Fraternity and the other one."

Brandie, as the Marquess was known to his friends, had obviously been drinking even though it was barely noon. "Parlez –vous Froggy?" he asked, stumbling against the stable door and scattering ash from the end of his cigar.

"You," said Lord Harry, addressing Peter, "get this fellow out of here before I lose my temper. Does he not know who I am?"

Before Peter could respond, John Graves appeared at the back of the crowd. He addressed Lord Harry, directly.

"My Lord, your guests are asking for you. I understand that Lady Frasier and her daughters have arrived ahead of a 'large party'."

Lord Harry now scowled at John.

"You need to keep the staff in better order," he declared. "They need to be more smart about it when I come to see my horses"

"Hear, hear!" said the Marquess, pulling himself up to his full height.

The stable-lads shuffled and looked at the ground as John Graves showed no sense of having heard the remark. Failing to provoke a reaction, Lord Harry addressed his friend.

"Get a move on, Brandie!" he urged, "I need to attend to my guests."

Fixing his eye on John but with a voice raised to address the crowd, he added:

"But I will be back, at my convenience, to inspect my stables and my horses, whenever and howsoever I choose."

Peter and Fabrice were left standing, shoulder to shoulder, in the stable doorway.

A GOOD WORKER

Fabrice had refused a section of the former dairy that now gave accommodation to the stablemen. Instead, he had cleared the hay loft in the lean-to where the comical horse was stabled and had quickly established a sense of order. Within a day, a rag rug had been laid across the floor and an old door had found a new use, straddled across two feed bins, as a writing desk. Jem had helped heave an old couch up into the loft and a basket chair, last seen in the conservatory, along with a stool and a dressing table with a pitted mirror had also appeared by some means unbeknown to the housekeeper. Fabrice had eaten with the men and had stumbled into their favour by attempting thanks in English and observing the strict but unspoken rules of seniority that existed "below stairs". Peter himself had pronounced him "welcome". He had pointed out the bathhouse and introduced him to the fearsome Mrs Grady, who was head of the laundry: her staff of five laundry maids, indistinguishable one from the other in the haze of steam and soap suds that continually hung in the air.

It seemed to be accepted that Hidalgo would fall to the handler's care, at least until the stallion was trained to the rein. Fabrice had fitted the saddle himself – revising the padding until there was no danger of pressure or rub. Hidalgo had fretted at the tightness of the girth and the stirrups that glanced his sides but Fabrice kept up the daily routine until horse and rider moved as one around the ménage.

Introducing Hidalgo to the bit was another matter. Fabrice tried warming the metal in a bucket of water; he tried various styles, materials and widths but Hidalgo fussed and danced about and then did his best to evade the bit once the bridle was in place.

Peter approached the paddock where Fabrice was working with the horse and was greeted with great courtesy by Nolly, who was casting an experienced eye over the proceedings from the shade of a copper beech. The pair of them watched Fabrice as he used his seat and legs to bring Hidalgo "up-together" and correct his stride.

Nolly shielded his eyes with his cap and looked across at horse and rider.

"He's a worker, I'll say that for him. He's been up at dawn and bed at dusk the whole month that he's been here. He's a strong un as well; throwing up the bales with the best of 'em. Not that I couldn't do the same if I was allowed."

Peter smiled and shook his head. This was an old complaint of Nolly's and Peter was no more going to ask the frail old man's help in clearing the barns than he was going to offend him by suggesting that he wasn't up to it.

"That there stallion's got him beat, though," chortled Nolly. "He'll do aught in the world for him, but he won't take that bit!"

"Perhaps old age and guile will work where youth and patience fail?" suggested Peter and he showed Nolly the bit and bridle that was slung over his arm.

"I don't consider you as old, Mr Robinson," responded Nolly, looking up at the powerful figure of the head stableman as he rose to leave, "but I do knows that you have shown a bit of guile in your time and that's a fact."

Peter entered the paddock as Fabrice brought Hidalgo to the gate. He held the bridle up for inspection and fingered the halter that Hidalgo had condescended to accept in place of reins. Fabrice responded with a Gallic shrug and upturned hands. Very slowly, Peter moved to Hidalgo's head. He showed the horse the bridle and Hidalgo snickered at the smell. The bit was a simple snaffle, dulled with age and the bridle was soft and pliant as a silk scarf. Hidalgo whinnied and looked around, he nosed into Peter's outstretched hand, nuzzling the bit with his lips. Peter moved the bit between the horse's teeth and let him chew. He gently lowered the bridle over the ears and fixed the browband. Finally, with a gentle stroke of the mane, Peter fastened the cheek straps and smiled.

Fabrice stood in amazement.

"He wouldn't do it for you, but he'll do it for Gloriana," laughed Peter. "It's her old bit and bridle that he's taken to – I thought he might. Just like he'll take to her, even though she's old enough to be his mother!!"

"Gloriana?" exclaimed Fabrice, clapping Hidalgo on the shoulder. "Oui, c'est toujours la femme, mon ami - always the woman, yes?"

Hidalgo had already been put out in the field with Gloriana. The mare was in season and, after some dangerous-looking rearing and squealing, with the odd near-kick for good measure, the two had cantered off together, tails in the air; Hidalgo prancing alongside the gleaming dark bay mare.

"They will make the most amazing foal," said Peter as they took Hidalgo back round to the stables, "but it's Princess that concerns me at the moment" and he motioned Fabrice to walk with him.

Princess was being cared for by Simon, Peter's deputy. He reported her to be well but "acting as if it were time". Concerned, Simon had brought her in, even though the full eleven months were some way off. Fabrice nodded at Simon and bent to inspect the mare, checking her udders, and looking for signs of a temperature. It was a maiden pregnancy and she was very large. Fabrice felt the belly and looked up at Peter.

"I'll leave a message for the vet to come by when he's checking on the Highland cattle, early next week. I'd look in on her myself before then but I'm in Swanton over night and may well not return until after the weekend."

Fabrice stepped forward. "I go nowhere, Mister Robinson. I can help."

Peter looked towards his Deputy who looked relieved rather than affronted.

"I am help you, yes?" Fabrice asked Simon, as the two shook hands.

It was the second night of Peter's absence that Jem woke Fabrice to tell him that his help was needed. Princess had gone into labour toward midnight and was circling and then rolling on the ground as if trying to turn the foal. Princess was now exhausted and the birth had ground to a halt. Following quickly in the light of Jem's lantern, Fabrice studied the scene in the stable. Simon's jaw was set tight with concentration and he was covered in sweat. His hands were inside the mare, but the foal was breech. Fabrice began to gently massage the mare's sides, in time with the contractions. Jem, wide-eyed with fear and lack of sleep offered to help but both men shooed him away and forced the mare back onto her feet, with Simon holding her head. The mare moaned and gazed round at the two men, her sides heaving and her breath coming out in strange rasping barks. Finally, she shuddered down the whole length of her body and with an unearthly piercing sound she breathed out from the depths of her belly as Fabrice managed to grab the hind legs. Fabrice laid the rimy body next to the mare. The mare turned and nuzzled at the damp bundle, whinnying softly. His eyes were still glued together and his head hung down. Fabrice held him out to the mare and she licked her newborn's head, gently butting the body with her nose. Fabrice cleared the foal's nostrils and blew. He would give him five minutes to get to his feet. Simon glared at Fabrice and motioned to the mare. He wanted to check the placenta and did not want a stillborn foal getting in the way. The foal lifted his head. He pushed up on his knees but the hind legs skittered and fell. Then, suddenly, he was up. Alive and trying to feed. The two men exchanged a glance of pure joy.

The vet arrived later in the day and declared both mare and colt to be doing well. Since Peter had not yet returned, he went in search of John Graves.

"Your stable hands did well," he said. "The mare could have torn and she would never have foaled again."

"They tell me it was mostly the gipsy's doing."

"Hmm, he seems to be lending a hand in any number of ways. He's also endeared himself to a couple of the local farmers who would never have called on my services but seem happy to deal with him. I hear that he is also bottle-rearing an orphaned filly here at New Hall. He's taken her in with his own horse and won't let anyone near. Apparently, he tried to make a bargain with His Grace, offering to stay on longer if he could keep her?"

John raised a wry eyebrow. "Hmm, while His Grace was speaking with Lady Frasier, as I understand it! Needless to say, her Ladyship was not amused – but His Grace decided it was fair and right: since no-one else had given the animal any chance of living through the night. His Grace has a good heart and a fine brain. He'll be sorry to lose the handler now that Gloriana is in foal. Hidalgo is becoming very proprietorial and difficult. Giving the Frenchman a reason to stay was both generous and clever."

"My daughter has been anxious to come and see the latest arrival," he continued. "Are mother and son sufficiently settled to allow that?"

"As if I could deny your daughter anything," replied the vet, in a voice too low to catch. "That would be perfectly acceptable," he said, aloud, to John.

THE LULLABY

Marianne breathed deeply as she entered the stables, drawing in a heady mix of sugar-smelling malt and straw and sunshine. Princess had been moved to the end of the stalls and Prince, the colt, was with her. The mare snuffled and chuntered and moved closer to her colt. Marianne peered at them through the dappled haze, bars of sunlight glinting on the honey-coloured straw and reflecting off the windows, set high in the wall. The colt was focussed on his feed, not even turning to note her arrival. Marianne stayed totally still but whispered softly to the mare, praising her beauty and her cleverness. She was wary of horses and viewed them from a distance but mother and son had her entranced and she was filled with a sense of overwhelming well-being.

"You love your baby, don't you?" she whispered. "You keep him close by your side."

Marianne felt tears catch in her throat and wondered at her own reaction. Silently, she climbed onto a mounting block and held the window-opening to steady herself. From this vantage point, she could see the colt's mesmerised face as he nuzzled for food and watch the mare's slow breathing as she nursed her son.

Through the window came the sound of singing; distant and sweet, carrying across the yard. Marianne froze like a deer sensing danger and the mare snorted in recognition. The song was well-known to her. It was the song of her childhood. A lullaby sung by her mother and never heard since. Her tears began to flow more freely. Dropping to the ground, she followed the sound out of the stables and across the yard – over to the disused hay-barn with the lean-to roof. Suddenly, the singing stopped and then renewed, getting louder as she reached the hay barn's door. Marianne pushed softly on the latch and peered through the opening. Fabrice was lying in the stall along with Belle and the orphaned filly: his head was on Belle's neck and the filly's head was resting in his lap. The straw was banked up the sides of the stall and the three lay deep in the hollow as Fabrice lullabied the filly and marked time with a stroke of Belle's multicoloured mane.

"How dare you sing that song!" Marianne blurted out, in French, barging in the door and causing all three to start. The filly struggled to her feet and made a noise closer to a lamb than a foal while the phlegmatic Belle sighed in annoyance.

"Stand still!" replied Fabrice, in a peremptory manner. "I don't tell you what you may and may not sing and I don't come into places where I am not invited. What do you think you are doing?"

He too got to his feet and squinted at Marianne as she stood outlined in the doorway, with the sunlight at her back. Belle shook her mane and stared – deciding that she was too comfortable to move.

"You've frightened the foal," he declared, moving to one side so that he was less blinded by the light. "What have you got to say for yourself?"

His hair was full of straw and his beard bristled with anger. Marianne drew herself up to her full height.

"I might well ask you the same," she said. "Sprawled out in the stable when you should be working - and mocking me with my mother's song."

Despite her wish to gain the upper hand, Marianne could not hold back the tears.

"It is you, you who have frightened me!" she wailed.

Picking up her skirt, she ran from the barn, letting the

door swing to. Fabrice plunged through the straw to the doorway but the stable yard was empty and Marianne was nowhere to be seen.

Her cheeks flushed and tears smarting her eyes, Marianne ran for cover. Darting behind the stable block, she sped alongside the garden wall and pushed against an arched gate, half-obscured by ivy. The cool of the kitchen garden welcomed her. Regimented rows of produce ran wall-to-wall with not a weed in sight. At the far end, one of the gardeners was setting up a line of canes. Keeping to the shade of the wall, Marianne skirted round the plot and out the other side. The glass houses – some with newly whitewashed panes to filter out the summer sun – glimmered in the heat. The first of the doors stood open and the smell of tomato leaves edged out on the breeze. Marianne quickly slipped inside. The air was moist and heady as she moved further in. In the middle was a rustic bench: used for resting and for potting up the seedlings. Marianne claimed its sanctuary as if it were a feather sofa. Now, at last, she could cry. Images of the foal mixed with the remembered strains of the lullaby. Her chest rose but the tears would not come. Only the anger remained. She blushed at having run away and stamped her foot as she determinedly re-traced her steps. Bolstering up her courage to confront the rude young man and rehearsing the peremptory tone in which she would take him to task, she stepped back out into the sunlight and collided with the portly paunch of an astounded Lord "Brandie" Brandon, Marquess of Kinshire.

"I say," he stuttered, taking in her pink cheeks and plain but well-made cotton dress. "I don't believe I've had the pleasure." He beamed at Marianne with what he held to be his most becoming smile. Marianne moved back a pace but kept her eyes on his.

"I'm dashed if you're not the prettiest little thing I've seen since I've come to the country," declared a now delighted Brandie as he slithered into the doorway to get a closer look.

His blotchy face and red-rimmed eyes appeared round the edge of Marianne's straw hat. She felt his hot, moist breath on her neck and flinched, almost imperceptibly. Brandie, quite literally, licked his lips and raised a long-nailed finger to his chin as he beamed at Marianne.

"Don't be shy. You're not frightened of old Brandie are you?"

"Certainly not," said Marianne, confusing him once again with her Queen's English and her disparaging look.

From the corner of her eye, she saw a movement, close at hand.

"Mr Grantham!" she cried, raising her hand in greeting. The Head Gardener looked surprised to see her but nonetheless approached whilst courteously removing his cap.

"I believe this gentleman is lost, Mr Grantham. Would you be able to help him?" Brandie glowered at the old man and scuffed his feet together.

"I can do without your help," he said, with a swagger.

"If that is the case, I will gladly accept it," said Marianne. "I'm feeling quite unwell with the heat and would be grateful for an escort back to the house. Mr Grantham, if you would?"

With a bow of the head to Brandie, the old man moved to her side. "It would be my pleasure, Miss Marianne."

A NEWLY LAUNDERED PILLOW

It was not until evening that Marianne discovered who the singer was or, indeed, the full identity of the noisome Brandie. She and her father had been invited to join Lady Wellesden in the music room to view a new piano she had ordered from Berlin. Lady Wellesden suffered indifferent health and as her eyesight became increasingly poor, she spent more time with her music and rarely attended formal events. Music was her consolation and her pleasure and she had long thought of Marianne as her protégé. She had "discovered" Marianne by hearing her sing at the annual harvest supper and was even more pleased to learn that Marianne was a keen pianist. For her part, Marianne delighted in the exquisite instrument that Lady Wellesden could now only play by memory.

John Graves, in his Sunday best, sat to one side as his daughter described the peculiarities of the piece of music that Lady Wellesden had had sent from town. Although she could no longer read the notes, Lady Wellesden had a strong sense of pitch and rhythm and was an avid supporter of the new. Her latest find was Claude Debussy, a French composer who flouted tradition and had been dismissed by some as a madman.

Marianne was peering at the score.

"I think I have it," she said, with a toss of the head and an unconscious stretching of her fingers. Hesitant at first, Marianne played with quiet skill and delicate feeling. The dream-like phrases of "L'après-midi d'un faune" blended into the still night air and Lady Wellesden's face showed some of its former beauty as she listened, enraptured. As the last note faded, both she and John took an inward breath before breaking into applause.

Lady Wellesden turned to the proudest of fathers.

"She is a credit to you, Mr Graves. And her talent deserves a wider audience."

John smiled and shook his head, his natural reticence disallowing praise even for his well-loved daughter.

"Will you now sing for me, my dear?" continued Lady Wellesden. "Perhaps another French composer?"

Marianne knew the very thing and stayed in a romantic vein. But their mood was on the verge of interruption. Footsteps approached from the hallway as Harry and Brandie swung into the room:

"This is where you've been hiding!" declared Harry, before stopping in his tracks and causing Brandie to collide into the back of him. Lady Wellesden looked up sharply.

"Mother, I do apologise, I thought we had discovered the Miss Frasiers. We have not seen them since dinner and when we heard the music …" Harry looked across at Marianne and received a nod of recognition in return.

Lady Wellesden shook her head and smiled.

"Only someone with your untutored ear could mistake this divine recital as coming from the Miss Frasiers! No, no. It is just myself, Marianne and Mr Graves trying out some very daring, and very complex, music from a new composer."

"Daring, eh?" said Brandie, moving into the light and leering at Marianne.

"I believe the Miss Frasiers are in the garden room," Lady Wellesden continued. "You could ask them to join us but Debussy is not to everyone's taste."

"And we must be going," said John, who had already risen as their Lordships entered the room.

Lady Wellesden sighed. "It is becoming rather late," she

agreed as she stood and turned toward them. "It just leaves me to thank you and bid you good night."

Brandie coughed and stepped forward. Detecting the movement, Lady Wellesden hesitated.

"I'm so sorry," she said. "How remiss of me. Mr Graves, Marianne, you already know my son but may I introduce his friend Lord Brandon, the Marquess of Kinshire."

John bowed and Marianne curtsied. Lord Brandon stepped forward as if to speak but father and daughter had already taken their leave of her Ladyship and were determined to respect her need to rest. They left the room without further ado but they were followed by the sound of Brandie's urgent whispers as he rudely quizzed his friend about "that girl Marianne".

Meantime, Marianne was pleased to have avoided being subjected to more of Lord Brandon's salacious stares.

"Ugh," she grimaced, squeezing her father's arm. "A Lord he may be but a gentleman, he is not!" Her father wondered at her vehemence but he did not question her.

"That is the second horrid man I have encountered, today," she continued. "The first was no gentleman, either – a stable hand of some kind – but a stable hand who spoke French."

"The Gipsy Rover: I'll bet," said her father, amused by her querulous face.

"Gipsy Rover! Don't tease," she said and then the mystery became clear.

"Ah, he's the horse handler! I've heard about him and I've seen him in the paddock. Gipsy Rover is right. He may well charm the horses but he is the rudest man I've ever come across. It seems as if he lives in the stable along with the animals and I think he better stay there." Catching her father's eye, she excused her own pertness. "At least that explains the French," she reflected as they hurried indoors.

Back in the main house, the Marquess of Kinshire was puffing and blowing and grabbing at Harry's sleeve to try and slow him down as they strode back through the Long

Room, still in search of the Miss Frasiers.

"But that's her – the very one I was telling you about! The same little filly that was casting her eye over me this afternoon"

Harry snorted. "She seems to have cooled towards you by this evening."

"Nonsense, old chap. It's all part of the game. What do you think the daring song was for – and French, eh? Juicy little French filly, what?"

Harry finally lost patience and grabbed his coat sleeve back from Brandie's clutches.

"A little French filly who is the daughter of my grandfather's Estates manager and a favourite of my mother. You should stay below stairs or try harder with the likes of the Miss Frasiers, Brandie. The former will not complain and the latter will not notice. Marianne Graves falls into neither category."

Brandie reached into his coat pocket and rustled some notes in Harry's face:

"We'll see", he said. "She may have her airs and graces: but, importantly, I have more than enough money to pay for them!"

Harry turned round to his friend, shaking his head but then appeared to think better of it and held out his hand.

"Well, since you're so flush and eager to please, you can let me have a little just to tide me over. There's the matter of a wager: debt of honour and all that. Foxy Foxton's getting uppity again and it's your fault that we took the bet in the first place."

Brandie rustled the notes and made as if to put them away but then thrust them at his friend.

"It was worth it though, eh? The badger gave as good as he got and Foxton's little bitch is a star in the making! Makes you wonder where he gets them from, eh? Badgers in the heart of London! Foxy Foxton. Fox, indeed – he lives up to his name and no mistake!"

THE BOATING PARTY

A mid-summer stillness held New Hall in its thrall. Even the bird song seemed distant and the horses moved noiselessly through the long grass that shimmered as they passed.

A whisper-thin mist, the herald of another perfect day, had barely left the lawns but Harry was already pacing about the terrace, looking edgy and cross. The plan had been to take a boat out on the lake with the Miss Frasiers (their Mamma having declined the invitation). The boat had been laden with the softest, silken cushions and deep-fringed parasols while an ornate picnic table had been set up under the shade of the trees on the larger island, at the far end of the lake. Brandie had been the plan's keenest supporter and yet he was nowhere to be found. Looking from the terrace, Harry could see the Miss Frasiers, the flounce of their dresses like the slow, colourful beat of butterfly wings, as they meandered through the meadow to the landing stage.

With a "view –halloo", Brandie appeared round the corner of the terrace steps:

"Where the devil have you been?" expostulated Harry. "This is deuced annoying of you!"

Brandie put a finger to his lips and sniggered:

"Just seeing to my laundry, old chap. You know I like to check the freshness myself." He licked the spittle from his lips and caressed the lines of his shirt against his body.

Harry grabbed hold of Brandie's arm and pulled him in the direction of the boat.

"Well just don't let Mrs Grady catch you, that's all I can say. It's her laundry and her laundry-girls."

"That's what you think! At least one of them is mine! Plump little Jemima, soft as a newly laundered pillow. Hey, did you hear that, Harry? Wait for me, old chap! Soft as a newly laundered pillow. A newly laundered pillow don't you see – Poetic, what?"

The eldest Miss Frasier, Lady Frasier of Runcorn, was an heiress in her own right and knew her own worth. Tall and willowy, her appearance was only marred by a slightly sallow complexion and thin lips that were often pursed in boredom. She was being put in Harry's way and she knew it. More importantly, so did he and whilst he was not ecstatic about the match, he had decided to view it as a business deal and he recognised that, as business deals go, this one was beneficial.

Lady Frasier's sister, Sophia, was the prettier of the two and the more flamboyant. She declared herself to be devoted to the Finer Arts. She swooned at the thought of Rossetti and styled herself on the pre-Raphaelites, adopting rather more floating gowns than were properly fashionable and insisting on flowery adornments of all kinds. At her insistence, the boat had been draped with lilies and as they pulled out onto the lake she began quoting from the Lady of Shallot.

Harry had taken his jacket off and was at the oars while Brandie sat in the prow.

"For God's sake, don't fidget so," said Lady Frasier, scowling, as Brandie waved his arms towards the island.

"Avast there, me hearties. We're pirates: not your lovesick knights, Sophia. Let's have a bit of rape and pillage."

Sophia squealed and a wry smile momentarily passed across her sister's face.

Sophia took the pins out from her chignon and released a cascade of auburn hair onto her shoulders. She pouted at her sister:

"Oh do perk up, Portia. It's a glorious day. We are in the magic kingdom and you are not going to spoil it for me."

Harry drew in the oars and they floated, listening to the

lapping of the water. Two small islands lay ahead of them, separated from the pasture beyond by a short strip of water. The smaller island was closely cloaked in trees and bracken, right down to the water's edge thus their picnic had been set up on the larger, more distant island. Only thirty yards across, it nonetheless had a small beach where they could easily get ashore.

To prolong the trip, Harry set to row between the two, gliding in a softly curving figure of eight that took them into slow-moving eddies that brushed the side of the boat. As they approached the smaller island, the shade of its little copse enclosed them in a secret shade and even Brandie fell silent.

Harry wielded the oars with skill, his manly display gaining the desired recognition from the seemingly languorous Portia. As they rowed out of sight of the house, they could see the horses grazing in the meadows to their left and the beginning of a heat haze rising off the lake. Lulled by the stillness, they lay back and listened to the hushed lilt of the water and the relaxed creaking of the timbers and they too breathed a sigh. Suddenly, a high-pitched whinny and the smack of water sliced into the enchanted air. The boating party started and exclaimed.

"What the devil!" muttered Brandie, shuffling further forward to see past the trees.

Eyes glittering, Brandie snorted and his suppressed laughter threatened to upset the boat as he wriggled round to whisper to the group.

"Horse and rider in the water, ladies, on the starboard bow. No cause for concern: man and beast swimming comfortably" and he burst into wheezy guffaws as he clamped his hand tightly over his mouth.

The party could now all see where he was pointing. Just off the larger island, facing back to the water meadows beyond, were a foal and a man; swimming side-by-side and playing in the shallows.

The foal was quick to notice the intruders and snickered

in fear. The swimmer had not yet spotted them but half rose from the water, looking back at the island to find the cause of the foal's reaction. His near-naked body shimmered in the sun and the ladies gasped.

Harry started to manoeuvre backwards as Brandie struggled to his feet, rocking the boat frantically from side to side and causing the Miss Frasiers to protest in alarm.

With operatic gusto, Brandie hailed the swimmer.

"Hoy, you there, in the water! There are ladies present! What the devil do you think you're doing?"

The swimmer ducked back under and headed into deeper water. Harry, more angry than alarmed, ordered Brandie to sit down. He then stood up himself and addressed the man.

"I am Lord Wellesden. How dare you offend my guests in this way? Leave here, immediately."

The boat was drifting closer to the swimmer as the filly swirled around him, blowing at the water and chuntering. The swimmer was now standing to his waist in water and made as if to bow. Sunlight scattered off the water droplets that were raining from his hair and glanced off his arms and chest.

"Excusez-moi, Milord, Mesdames. Je suis désolé. I do not know that you are here. We are going this minute," he declared. True to his word, he immediately struck out for the further shore, with the filly mewling in his wake.

The swimmer and the foal reached the meadow as Harry cut in through the gap between the islands. The Misses Frasier, despite a comely display of blushes and giggles, looked back towards the further shore.

"That's a damn fine-looking foal," said Brandie, as the filly trotted off into the meadow, at Fabrice's shoulder. "She has the making of a first-rate runner when she's fully-grown. I'd think you'd want to keep her in mind, old man."

Lady Frasier caught her sister's eye. Sophia sent a silent message in return and then looked past her sister, sideways, to the meadow. Her gaze was not directed at the foal.

A BREAK IN THE WEATHER

A break in the weather had prevented much of the activity John Graves had planned for the day. He met with the Estate's staff, early, to re-direct their efforts. Mr Grantham sent the gardeners to the glass houses: clearing and disinfecting after the early crops; Mr Robinson ordered a complete stock-take of tack and the various day-labourers went off to the barns to make ready for the first of the hay. John would use the time to go to Newbold farm. Robert Baker had bought the farmhouse from the Estate and was gradually buying a share of the land.

"Do you fancy coming along to Newbold?" he asked Marianne when she appeared at his office door. "I'll keep the hood up so you won't get wet"

"I'd like to come with you, Papa, but I am working on my bonnets with Amy. We have them all out in my room and the dressmaker arrives just after lunch. This is the effect I am after. How will that look at the harvest supper?"

John glanced at the fashion frames his daughter held out for his approval and smiled indulgently.

"I was worried that I might not be back for supper but it seems as if you will be fully occupied. Has Amy put my cape out by the door? She may be good with bonnets but her memory for daily work leaves a lot to be desired."

Marianne went out to the porch to wave her father off. The rain had settled to a drizzle but the sky was surprisingly dark. Over at the Hall, lights showed in the library and in several rooms that gave on to the terrace.

Out of the line of view from the terrace and tucked behind the belt of trees which ran alongside the main drive, their cottage shared the same stone as the house. With just one room for visitors and John's office at the back, there was still ample space for father and daughter to pursue their own interests. Marianne had a day room where she had a small piano and a writing desk. This led to her sitting room which was her retreat at evening-time and where she was often joined by her father.

Marianne had few friends in England, having been educated in France and "above her station" as some would have it. Doctor Maltby's daughter, Anne, had proved to be a kindred spirit and they had attended concerts in the nearby town and shared books and intense conversation but the friendship had been interrupted by Anne's engagement to a cavalry officer – a distant cousin whom she had re-met just last year. In despite of a limited number of close social contacts, Marianne never seemed to have a moment to herself, however, and was looking forward to a day indoors.

In the event, the dress-maker had taken up the greatest part of Marianne's day and it was becoming dark by the time her father returned. Only August and already the nights were drawing in and a scattering of leaves had fallen from the trees. Father and daughter had supper together and withdrew to the sitting room. But Marianne's hopes of a quiet cup of tea and an account of life at Newbold were soon shattered. A desperate pounding on the door drew John back up to his feet.

"Mr Graves, Mr Graves! Please come on to the house, as quick as you may. Mrs Grady is beside herself and she do not know who else to call. Help us, Mr Graves. Please come on to the house."

Mr Graves set off at a run, fast on the heels of the distraught young woman. Amy stood in the doorway, looking to Marianne for explanation but Marianne could never have imagined the sight that her father was about to witness.

In one of the many outhouses to the rear of the main hall, Mrs Grady was kneeling on the floor weeping over a girl. She rocked and nursed her as she would a baby. The girl moaned like a frightened animal, catching her breath instead of crying and burying her face further into Mrs Grady's shoulder.

"Oh, Mr Graves. Thank God you've come. I don't know what to do for the best. Should I get a doctor? Should I alert the Hall? Send for the police? Just look at this poor lamb!"

She turned the young girl's face round to the light and John flinched at the bruises and cuts. As the girl twisted back into Mrs Grady's arms, he also saw the stain of blood that was seeping through the linings of the girl's dishevelled skirt.

"The poor mite's been like this since I arrived. Too shocked to speak and won't let go of me. Mr Grady's off down to the village for her mother so she should be here any minute. At least we have the beast that did this to her safe and sound. I gave him such a wallop with the soaking pan I near as knocked him senseless. Then me and Sadie locked him in the starch-room store."

Sadie, red in the face from running for help, now blushed damson as her part in the rescue was explained.

"One of your men – do you see - Mr Graves or we might well have called out Mr Knight? I'm still not sure whether we should send for him – or should we contact Mrs Fells? Mr Knight's head of household but it's the housekeeper who most has the charge of us domestics. I just don't know what I should rightly do?"

Mrs Grady looked, wild-eyed, to John for guidance. With the utmost care, she laid the victim on the floor. The injured girl was now entirely silent and her eyes were staring open but they gave no sign of life.

Running in ahead of Mr Grady, the girl's mother arrived. She wore a work coat pulled on over her night clothes and her cries rose to a wail when she saw her daughter lying prostrate on the floor.

"Jemima, Jemima! – It's me, my darling. What have they done to you, my sweetling? Jemima, my baby!" She crouched down by the girl and stroked her hair, pointing to the bruises in amazement and despair.

"We need to get her home," said Mrs Grady: taking back some of her usual authority. "Mr Grady will take you in the cart and Sadie will ride with you and help you with her at the other end."

"I'll get a message to the doctor so he should be with you soon after you arrive," said John. "Is there anyone else you need us to contact or any other help we can give you?" Jemima's mother spun round to where John stood: not seeming to have noticed there were other people in the room.

"Mr Grady mentioned fetching the Police, sir, and we mayn't do that, not if you want to help. Please, don't have the police attend. I beg you not to add to my girl's shame. Who's going to want her when they hear of this? As few of them as can be should be told. She must be spared the tattle of the world. God knows, she's damaged enough."

"But a crime has been committed and, as I understand it, the criminal is caught. The full weight of the law can now be brought to bear."

"The full weight of the law will crush my daughter right along with her attacker. Please, sir. If her father were alive, we'd need no law. My daughter's hurt would be revenged no matter how. I will not let her face the court: I will not let her bear the shame."

John bowed his head and Mr Grady scooped the girl up from the floor. Jemima's mother clasped her hands in supplication and pleaded in turn with the silent group.

"I want you all to swear before our God above that what you have seen here stays within these walls. Doctor Maltby is as kind a man as any in this world. He knows full well to keep a secret and I need his help, but no-one else must know: you all must promise me!"

John drew her outstretched hands towards him and

looked steadily in her face:

"I will promise not to act without your leave and I will promise not to speak a word outside this room. But I cannot let the matter rest. We have a monster in our midst and he must not be allowed to go unpunished." John's decision met with nods and promises from the others and the semi-conscious girl was carried to the cart, now clutching limply to her mother.

Mrs Grady led the way down the side entry. John squared up to the store-room door and Mrs Grady turned the key. He need not have worried that the rapist could escape. Sadie had bound him hand and foot and he had a gag between his teeth. Blood had now congealed across his temple and lay matted in his curly hair. A ribbon of blood had run down to the gag and there were smears of blood across his shirt.

"My God, it's Dupres!" John Graves exclaimed, as he knelt beside the inert body. With untypical roughness, he removed the gag and ropes but Fabrice merely groaned and stirred. John bent low and checked the handler's breathing.

"He'll keep till morning," he decided. "I'll be back at eight, with Doctor Maltby if he can join me. The girls are not in work, tomorrow, I presume, Mrs Grady?"

"Sadie and myself will sometimes work a Saturday if guests are due but the Frasiers left today and no one is expected for the next few days."

"Till tomorrow, then, Mrs Grady. If you and Mr Grady will place some water and a bucket in our makeshift cell, we'll leave Dupres to come round in his own time. This storeroom door is strong enough to hold a bull and there's no-one here to hear him if he calls."

As John expected, his daughter had not gone to bed when he returned. Happily, Amy had had been sent off home. Pale and sleepy, Marianne nonetheless appeared in the hallway seconds after John had crossed the threshold.

"Papa, where have you been? What on earth is the matter?"

"I am sorry to alarm you my dear Chouchou. And I'm

sorry to return so late. I have come back via the village since there was a promise that I had to keep. I can now tell you what has happened over these last few hours but I must first swear you to absolute secrecy and warn you that it is a sordid and unhappy tale."

TRUTH WILL OUT

The next day, Dr Maltby joined them as they finished breakfast and all three set off towards the laundry: keeping close up to the garden walls. As they approached the storeroom Fabrice began to yell. His cries were in a gipsy-language French that even Marianne found hard to follow. With the help of Mr Grady, the three men brought Fabrice out from the makeshift cell, once more bound at hand and foot. His rage was incandescent and his voice rose to an even higher pitch when they were joined by Mrs Grady and the trembling Sadie.

"Calmez-vous, Monsieur," said Marianne, causing Fabrice to stop still in his tracks.

"Mademoiselle," he pleaded, in French, fixing his eyes on hers. "I have done nothing wrong. I startled her attacker and was going for help. Ask the girl. Ask the girl!"

Both John and Doctor Maltby had sufficient French for this response but needed Marianne to question further. Mrs Grady fixed the accused with a thunderous gaze snarling like a terrier pulling at a bone and Sadie's eyes were spiked with tears.

"He says, he's not guilty," explained John turning towards the witnesses.

"What was he doing here, then? Ask him that? Whose is all the blood that's on his shirt?" asked Mrs Grady, shaking with emotion.

Marianne put both questions to Fabrice. He looked down

at the blood and started to reply. Stopping, he suggested Marianne translate and he would tell them exactly what had happened, while they sent for the girl.

He reported that he had heard some screaming as he walked back from the stables and had tried to grab the man who was molesting the girl. The attacker had run off and the girl had fastened onto her rescuer's legs, pleading with him not to leave her. Just as he was bending down to pick her up, he heard a noise and was hit with something from behind. He then woke up much later with the blood from his wound dried onto his face and clothes.

"Ask the girl," he pleaded, in heavily-accented English. "Ask the girl!!"

"How is Jemima, Doctor?" asked Mrs Grady. "Can she tell us what went on here, yesterday?"

"I gave her a sedative to make her sleep and she was still not properly awake when I called by, just now. She is feverish and in a lot of pain. She was talking about brandy and got most agitated when we could not understand. It may be that the attacker tried to drug her with some spirits but there was no trace of smell and her cuts and scratches show that she was putting up a fight and fully conscious. There's no way I want to bring her from her bed. There's more to be discovered from the attacker. Please tell Dupres I wish to examine him, Miss Marianne"

Dr Maltby sniffed Fabrice's hair and clothes and looked carefully at the wound.

"No sign of brandy here, either — and no other scratches: just the wound. It makes no sense at all."

"There may be more sense than we think," said Marianne. Her face was flushed and she reached out for her father's hand before directing a further question to Fabrice.

"The man you say attacked the girl, did you get a good look at him?"

Fabrice shook his head. "It was quite dark but he was stocky with light hair. He wore expensive clothes and smelled of wealth: not like a working man."

Drawing herself up to her full height, Marianne spoke firmly:

"Papa, I think Lord Brandon could well be of help with the investigation, if you and Dr Maltby could escort him here."

"Lord Brandon! What has he to do with this?"

"Papa, I promise you, he knows more than we think. We owe it to the gipsy to follow up on his defence."

"But Dupres never mentioned Lord Brandon."

"No, but Jemima did – she called him Brandie – It's the name he calls himself."

Doctor Maltby gasped as John wondered how on earth his daughter knew so much about Lord Wellesden's friend.

Shaking his head, the doctor moved across to John's side.

"I don't know how to go about this, Graves. What if Lord Brandon refuses to play ball?"

John Graves responded with a look of utter determination.

"The honour of New Hall is now at stake. This is therefore a matter for the Duke. We can be sure of both his probity and secrecy. I will see if his Grace will attend us here"

John set off for the house and, against her better judgment, Mrs Grady fetched food and drink and gave some to Fabrice, her husband having taken off the linen bands with which the prisoner had been bound. Draining the water but refusing any food, Fabrice stood aloof, glowering at his accusers.

It took some thirty minutes but when John returned, true to his word, he was accompanied by the Duke of Newton and Lord Brandon.

"What the deuce!" exclaimed his Lordship when he saw those present; excusing his language, as he registered the Duke's frown.

Lord Brandon strode into the middle of the room.

"So where's this chit that claims I've done her harm? Decided better of it, eh?"

"The girl is gravely ill, my Lord, and cannot describe her attacker, at this time," responded Dr Maltby.

His Lordship snorted. "I bet she can't. Not only have I never harmed a girl: I've never been near this place in my entire life. What would I be doing in a laundry?"

Sadie pulled at Mr Graves' sleeve.

"I took this from Jemima when she went to bed, last night. She had it so tight in her hand, it marked her flesh. I don't know whose shirt it come off but it don't look like it belongs to no gipsy"

John held out the pearl and turquoise shirt stud to the Duke and turned to Lord Brandon.

"Yours, my Lord?"

"How dare you?" shouted his Lordship, looking to the Duke for his support.

Doctor Maltby stepped into the beam of light that slanted through the door.

"May I ask you to remove your hat, my Lord?"

"My hat?" responded Lord Brandon. "Are you mad?" The Duke had no need to speak: his look drove Brandon to remove his hat.

"These scratches near your ear and in your hair, my Lord, would you tell us how you got them?"

"No I damn well won't. I've no need to explain myself to you. Just because some silly girl objects to a bit of harmless fun, there's no need to get all solemn and tight-lipped."

His Lordship turned towards the Duke and adopted a knowing air.

"She'd been more than ready, I can tell you. It is I who has been insulted. The little minx prinks and pouts and brings herself to my attention; leads me on and then cries wolf. It's women the world over, I'm afraid to say."

"She's fifteen, Your Grace," blurted Mrs Grady.

The Duke's face revealed disgust and decision. He clasped John Graves by the shoulder.

"I will deal with this from here. We can exact a kind of justice without taking this to court and shaming the poor girl further. I am a power to be reckoned with, without involving the Police."

The Duke of Newton raised his voice above Lord Brandon's protests. "I order you to leave my house at once and not return. Within the year, not one house in England will receive you. This is my determination and I am known to have my way, you despicable man."

John Graves grimaced as Lord Brandon left the room. He turned to face Fabrice and made to speak. Totally ignoring the stunned onlookers, Fabrice confronted Marianne. His white lips softened and he took her hand. Turning her clasped palm over, he left the suggestion of a kiss on her trembling fingers before dashing from the room, in tears.

HARVEST SUPPER

New Hall harvest supper was held on the first Friday in October. An invitation went to every worker and tenant on the Estate. A blind eye was even turned to a few "hangers-on" as Mr Knight, the Head of household staff, dubbed the young men and women who did not work on the Estate but were the sweethearts or fiancées of those who did.

Four massive marquees had been placed on the lawns overlooking the lake; one of which had its sides open and flooring laid for dancing. The kitchen and ground staff had been working flat out until late Thursday night but today was their chance to enjoy themselves. The Duke had ordered hog and lamb roasts from the butcher in Newbold and it was the butcher and his staff who would bring laden trays of fresh-roast meat to the well-worn trestle tables already set up in the marquees. By New Hall tradition, the senior staff were waiters at the harvest supper and were often joined by keen but unskilled helpers from the Duke's own family.

John and Marianne surveyed the scene. The day had been warm but there was enough hazy cloud to keep the chill from the air. A selection of breads, fruits and cheeses ran down the centre of the tables while trailing ropes of flowers and greenery cascaded from the tent poles. At the end of each trestle stood a hamper swathed in dampened cloths: smelling sweetly of vanilla and spice. Mrs Fells, the Housekeeper, had supervised the making of their contents herself: placing a pinny over her bombazine skirt and a bib over her starched, high-necked blouse. The younger staff had looked cowed as the Housekeeper had moved toward the floured bench at the centre of the kitchen but their high spirits soon returned since "she was acting just like someone normal" as a pot-boy declared, in an unfortunately audible whisper.

Marianne breathed in the smell of canvas and the heady notes of cider and elderflower. She and her father were on duty keeping jugs and glasses filled until the dancing started so her day dress would do well enough for now. Looking across the lake, she could see signs of the first arrivals from the farms and several female members of the household staff had come and peeked and run away again: not prepared to be the first at table.

By some unspoken rule, the tables filled up, like with like. A boisterous younger group jostled for places while trying not to be the first to sit. Small children were gathered together by the older girls and even the youngest left the safety of their mothers' skirts when they saw the half-sized tables in the dance tent: each place laid with a small striped box – the kind of box only seen before in the village sweetshop. The ladies' maids vied with the farmers' daughters in terms of dress and the occasional young beauty shone through, whatever her station.

Within the hour, full justice had been done to the roasted meats and the hampers had finally been uncovered to gasps of delight at the assorted jellies, creams and decorated puddings that were revealed. As the light grew dim, a variety of lamps were brought into play. Storm lamps, coach lamps, lamps used on more refined occasions when the Duke dined alfresco with his guests. The flames lit up faces already fired with laughter and the occasional suggestion of too much ale. As the first strains of music mingled with the general hubbub, mothers sought their younger offspring and fathers gave notice of one more hour to those allowed to stay for the start of the dancing.

The dance tent had the look of a pagoda, with Chinese

lanterns strung across the frame. The sides had been partly lowered to conserve the heat and a squeezebox ripened the sound of violins and flute. Mr Knight, as head of household staff, joined with Mrs Fells to lead the dance. Warmed by their efforts in serving food, they looked relaxed as they encouraged more couples to join them. Both had forsaken the stately attire that they adopted when on duty and both looked younger for it. The Duke's family withdrew but not before raising a glass to their staff and being rewarded with a mighty cheer.

As befitting the age and the standing of those on the floor, the musicians struck up a slow traditional air, part Scottish in its origins. John now partnered Mrs Knight and Marianne, in a dress of pale grey silk, the elegance of which belied its cost, had cajoled the Knights' eldest, Charlie, to join her in the dance. Taller than Marianne and with a courtesy modelled on that of his father, the young man blushed but did not draw attention to them both by protesting. He took her hand: pride vying with nervousness and joined the two sets of couples ranged down the centre of the marquee. Concentration gave him a serious look but as the dance progressed the promising youth and his lively partner drew all eyes to them and Charlie looked triumphant as he returned a radiant Marianne to her father when the music ceased.

Other couples now came on the floor. The speed and noise began to spiral, as the young men spun their partners hard, to make them squeal. The boarded floor vibrated and the air inside the tent thickened with the heat. Even Nolly performed a kind of clog-dance in the corner and the stable-lads gave him a round of applause. The Graves' maid, Amy, flew round in the sun-tanned arms of a farmer's son, trying to keep to time, in despite of her partner's earnest incompetence.

A cheer went up as Robert Baker and his Newbold herdsmen arrived with the Harvest Punch – sent down from the Hall. The dancers cleared the floor, stepping out of the tent to feel the chill of the October air or sitting at small tables where corn-dolly fans were put to good effect. The dancing would re-continue, later, but while the musicians got their breath and their fair share of the punch, the call went up for entertainment. Four of the grooms did a music-hall number and Mr Grady delivered a comic monologue to the dismay of Mrs Grady and the delight of all her staff. John and Robert sang a sea shanty and Marianne sang a local folk song with a chorus picked up by all present. At the far end of the marquee, a scuffle among the stablemen brought Fabrice to his feet and, before he could take cover, the stool on which he had been sitting was removed.

"I do not know the English song," he said, more in perplexity than protest.

"But I do," said Marianne, giving him a song sheet and a smile of encouragement. "Plaisir d'Amour has English words too?" he asked.

With John providing a mellifluous background, Fabrice and Marianne sang side by side: the one in French: the other in English. Their voices blended in the sweet refrain and the hysteria of the dance became a memory as sweethearts drew closer together and listened to the plangent tones. The young singers made a striking sight, singing for the joy of it: with no false modesty and just a touch of pride.

In the far corner of the tent: away from the lanterns, Lady Frasier shook her head in disbelief.

"If these are the servants at play, I can only say that they are too refined to be amusing."

"Be quiet, Portia," said her sister. "Hiding out here has to be better than bridge with mother and the baleful Bishop Hardy."

Lord Harry Wellesden stood back further from the light. The Frasier party had returned to New Hall earlier in the day and it was hard work playing host alongside his duties to the Harvest supper.

"I have commissioned the self-same style of dress as that, myself," Portia complained, pointing to Marianne. "And I was told I was the first in London to adopt the latest French design. What a nonsense! She looks like the Lady of the house rather than a servant and her singing partner looks like an alarming brigand."

Sophia smiled. Fabrice's Sunday best was in marked contrast to that of his fellows. His jacket was embroidered at the cuffs and collar and a sash of scarlet silk took the place of a cummerbund. Having bowed to the hearty applause, Fabrice escorted Marianne back to her seat. He left her not with a goodbye but with an invitation. In whispered French, he requested that she meet him at noon, the next day. Flurried by the arrival of Robert Baker to lead her back into the dance her eyes gave him the tacit acceptance he required and she turned to place her hand on Robert's arm.

THE GIFT

The arrangement had been to meet at the stable where Marianne had first met Fabrice on the day of the lullaby. Intrigued by the secrecy, she was also relieved to find Jem at the meeting place when she arrived. Jem stepped forward excitedly.

"Fabrice will not be long, Miss Marianne. He is just gone fetching your surprise."

Jem could not stop grinning and was rolling his eyes toward the stable door. As Marianne followed his wordless communication, Fabrice stepped out into the yard, leading a dappled pony, groomed to a shine and with ribbons plaited in her mane.

"I've called her Sage," he said, "because it means well-behaved in French and wise in English: and she is both. There's a superstition that you should not change a horse's name but since I bought her at the sales, she did not have a name. There's also a belief that if you give a horse a good name . . . ."

Marianne leaned forward and stroked the pink-white nose.

"She's lovely. I don't know why we call them greys when this one is so white. Her mane is the colour of iron, so perhaps that's the reason?"

Looking from one to the other, Jem cut through the French with a question in English:

"So you like her, Miss? Fabrice has made a good choice

for you?"

Fabrice scowled at Jem's question and Marianne's confusion.

"I am not yet saying the surprise!" he exclaimed in English, as all eyes turned toward him. Jem looked at his feet, chastened, and Marianne raised her eyebrows inviting further explanation.

"It's a gift for you, Miss Marianne - to thank you for your help when I was wrongly accused. I've tested her in every way and I'd trust her with my grandmother. She truly is Sage."

"But ... I... I cannot accept such a gift."

"It's the very least I could do. The Duke insisted that I accept some compensation from Lord Brandon. His Grace demanded that his Lordship pay for his lies as if he had gone to court for sentencing. He also demanded a much greater sum to help the victim. (I will not say her name in front of anyone even though we speak in French.) I understand that she and her mother have moved away to be closer to her sisters and further from the trauma."

Marianne glanced at Jem to see if he had any understanding and he took it as a cue.

"Just say that you like her, Miss. Fabrice's English does you proud: them books you give him must have helped tremendous. He can talk practical the same as you and me."

Fabrice smiled in response to Marianne's quizzical look.

"Jem's understanding that the gift was to thank you for the English lessons was provided by the stablemen themselves so I have just not disabused them. Please accept the pony. She cost me almost nothing. When I bought her she was skin and bone and full of worms. She was bound for the slaughterhouse. We have saved her."

Marianne began to smile:

"This is the first time that I've been offered a worm-eaten, cut-price gift that would really suit your grandmother" she said, mischievously.

Then, before Fabrice could bridle at her teasing, she

gently leaned against the pony's side and said in English:

"She's perfect and the fact that we have saved her makes her doubly precious."

Her smile turned from mischief into radiance as she shook Fabrice's hand.

"Thank you," she said.

THE YOUNG RIDERS

As Lady Wellesden's eyesight got worse her reliance on Marianne, for companionship, markedly increased. Her Ladyship had already persuaded John to have his daughter stay in England until the New Year: Tante Jeanne having been mollified by an invitation to spend "English Christmas" with her niece and brother-in-law.

Marianne's days had thus developed a routine: music, reading and excursions with Lady Wellesden in the morning and her own household duties after lunch: with a visit to Sage as a daily treat. John's diffidence about his daughter accepting the gift had been matched by his daughter's initial fear of being kicked or bitten. But as Marianne grew in confidence, John's misgivings were quietened by her delight at the pony and the pleasure she took in caring for her. He would have been much less happy if he had known that she had started having riding lessons. Not that Marianne had deliberately deceived him. She told herself that he didn't know because she had never thought that the lessons would continue so it was not worth worrying him. But now that she was improving she was determined to get better: not to ride in public or for display but as a point of personal honour and, if she dared admit it, to show Fabrice that she could master the skill.

Her first time on horseback had merely been to bring Sage back into fitness. Fabrice was too heavy for the little mare and Jem too tall. Perched side-saddle on the sure-footed pony's back, Marianne had felt excitement and a sense of rightness. Without thinking, she relaxed into the pony's rhythm, tracking round the improvised indoor school on a leading rein. Fabrice was a good and practised teacher. Peter, the Head Stableman, had encouraged Fabrice to give lessons to his boys whose attention if their father taught them was surprisingly poor. Fabrice was firm with the boys but forgiving while Peter's patience, legendary as it was with horses, did not seem to extend to his ten year old twins. The weekly lesson that all three had together was hilarious. The boys had no fear and vied with each other to best please Fabrice. In the face of their Cossack approach to riding, Marianne had adopted some of their attitude and a pair of their older brother's cast-off trousers that were exactly the right size. Riding astride just seemed to make more sense and, with her hair twisted up in a cap, Marianne looked barely older than the twins as they took on small jumps and practised riding bare-back, with no reins.

Their squeals and merriment had caught the attention of the Misses Frasier. Now officially engaged to Lord Harry, Portia was often at New Hall and her sister mostly accompanied her.

Peter looked embarrassed as Lord Harry entered.

"Is there anything I can help you with, my Lord? I thought the riding party had left?"

"Too wet for Lady Frasier, Robinson. We're confined to barracks, I'm afraid."

A keen and skilful rider, Lord Harry found it difficult to keep the regret from his voice. He looked across at the school. The riders were tracing trotting poles, hands raised above their heads like Indian braves saluting the sun.

"Are those your boys?" Lord Harry asked. "You must be proud of them. Who's your instructor?"

"The gipsy," breathed Sophia as she spotted Fabrice setting the jump higher.

The riders cantered round the outside of the school, their ponies snorting as the two boys tried to gain the lead. The twins' ponies cleared the jump almost in unison and all would have been well had one not clipped a pole on landing. A couple of paces behind the boys, Sage had addressed the jump in fine style but was about to land on a scattering of barrels and poles. Marianne checked her in mid-air and then gave with her hands. The sure-footed pony righted herself and swerved sideways. Marianne kept her seat almost by an act of faith and gave a whoop of relief as she landed clear of the poles. Her cap sailed off and landed at Fabrice's feet, as he rushed forward to check she was unharmed.

All four watchers had flinched as they saw the scene unravel and Peter's face had blanched. As Fabrice lifted Marianne to the ground, Portia laughed.

"Look, Wellesden, it's a girl! And you won't let me hunt with you for fear I'll slow you down. A girl in breeches! Maybe that's what I need to wear to convince you."

"Miss Marianne?" called Lord Harry, after the retreating figure of the girl whom he had spoken to only that morning as she had gently guided his mother around the orangery.

Lord Harry turned to glare at the Head Stableman

"I hardly think this is a suitable pastime for Mr Grave's daughter."

"I'm not sure her father knows about this," said Peter. "I think she means to surprise him."

"A girl after my own heart," declared Lady Frasier. "Her high spirits are to be applauded: not suppressed. No one will hear of this through me."

"Nor me," said Sophia, turning to Lord Harry and looking up from under her eyelids. "But ...... I wonder if you and your stableman would oblige me? This is a secret I wish to be part of – I too need an outlet for my high spirits!"

AN ARTFUL PUPIL

Fabrice was not easily persuaded to take another pupil but Peter made it clear that the request contained a hidden edge that made it more of an order. Sophia arrived alone and shrouded in a long grey cloak. A groom handed over a skittish Arab to Fabrice and Sophia removed the cloak to reveal hussar's trousers, held up with broad red braces over a fine lawn shirt.

"I want to ride like a man," she said as Fabrice cupped his hands for her to mount. "My sister can fly over hedges in a bundle of petticoats but that will not do for me."

Sophia immediately kicked the Arab into a high-stepping trot. She was not as good a rider as her sister but she had ridden since she was a child and was now executing some well-turned circles at the far end of the school. She cantered back, the Arab tossing his head and pulling at the rein.

"I want to do some jumping, now. Where are the poles?"

Fabrice brought the barrels and poles into the centre of the school without saying a word but made no attempt to set them up.

"Before the jump, I want you to do the stop," he said

Sophia looked him straight in the eye. "I am already doing the stop," she replied with a lazy insolence.

"I want you to do the canter and then you stop when I am saying to you. If you cannot do the stop: you cannot do the jump."

Sophia tossed her curls and set off round the school. She

looked across at Fabrice.

"When would you like me to stop?" she enquired as she rode dangerously close to him.

"When I say it," he replied, letting out a strange cry that pricked the Arab's ears. The Arab lengthened his stride as Sophia gathered up the reins. Fabrice let out a piercing ululation at which the Arab tossed his head and rolled his eyes. Sophia's colour rose and her foot reached for her lost stirrup. The Arab cantered in a frenzy, deaf to all suggestion.

"Stop!" said Fabrice as the Arab struggled to evade the bit. "Stop!" he repeated as the Arab threw in a buck. Sophia pulled at the reins viciously but the Arab continued round the school, heedless of her wishes. She had begun to slip slightly in the saddle as the Arab came round level with Fabrice. At that point, with a complete change of pitch, the handler called to the horse: a deep-throated, drawn-out note that was closer to a chant than a command. Twisting to keep Fabrice in his view, the Arab snorted, slowed down to a walk and circled to a standstill by Fabrice's shoulder.

"You did that on purpose!" said Sophia, close to tears.

"A clever horse need a clever rider, no? It is the control: always the control. The horse is big and strong than you. I am not wanting you to have hurt, my Lady."

Fabrice looked up at her; his eyes revealed concern and earnestness.

Sophia brought her foot across the pommel to turn and face Fabrice.

"Help me down," she said, holding out her arms.

As he set her on the ground and released her, Sophia threw a triumphant smile at Marianne who was standing, windswept, in the entrance to the barn. Marianne placed her basket of apples and carrots inside the doorway, turned on her heel and was gone, unnoticed by Fabrice who had his back to her. Still with an air of smug self-satisfaction, Sophia pointed to her cloak and waited for Fabrice to replace it on her shoulders.

"Tomorrow!" she ordered, daring Fabrice to gainsay her

and swept out of the arena with a theatrical swirl of the cloak. Alone in the school, Fabrice gazed at the floor. The Arab nuzzled the handler's shoulder and the handler rubbed his face into the horse's high-arched mane.

A NEW ACQUAINTANCE

The dinner at Dr Maltby's was in honour of their thirtieth wedding anniversary and Anne, their newly-married daughter, was returning to celebrate with them. Marianne was delighted at the thought of seeing her old friend again. She once more wore her dove-grey silk and her dark beauty caused something of a stir among the Maltby's eligible guests. Robert Baker was seated to her right with the new son-in-law's brother, James, to her left. Both of her dinner companions were keen to engage her in conversation. Robert updated her with his changes at Newbold and James proved to be an entertaining raconteur, regaling her with gossip from Dublin alongside that of London. Sitting opposite Marianne, Anne referred every topic of conversation to her taciturn but extremely dashing husband, Captain Dehan. The Captain had recently left the 4th Royal Irish Dragoons but he retained the glamour of the regiment, nonetheless. Whether from shyness or arrogance, he replied only to his brother's questions; turning his head from speaker to speaker but only responding with a slight and disconcerting frown. Anne was speaking of the King. She had been in London at the time of the Coronation four years ago and had been to this year's International Exhibition when the King visited in February. She had been delighted by the pomp and ritual.

"They stand need to celebrate with another war on the horizon," said Robert. "We lost two village lads to the Boers.

What has Africa got to do with the likes of us?"

Anne lightly clutched her husband's arm but directed her appeal to his brother.

"James, you'll support me in this, surely? The new King's reign is a time for rejoicing and Lord Lansdowne promised that the war in Africa is over."

"Lord Lansdowne!" snorted Robert as Marianne, who had noted the Captain's rising agitation, saw her chance to intervene.

"Gentlemen," she protested, with her sweetest smile, "I think we're being called to toast our hosts. Let's leave the bewildered state of the country to the politicians and raise a glass to the blessed state of matrimony."

James, Robert and the Captain rose to their feet with the others and Anne ran to the head of the table to embrace her parents.

Robert joined the ladies early after dinner and sought Marianne out to apologise.

"James told me that his brother was injured in the last months of the South African war. He has partly lost his hearing as a result and has had to leave the service. I feel a complete dolt bringing politics to the table. It's not as if the Irish are unequivocal in their support for the war: in spite of Lord Frederick Roberts' brigade. Young James Dehan sees the whole affair as being money-driven and trusts neither side – but there's lawyers for you. He can argue a case as well as any I've heard but I'm still not sure where his heart is."

As if he had heard his name, James appeared at the sitting room door.

"My sister-in-law tells me that you play and sing like an angel, Miss Graves. Let me escort you to the piano so as to calm my troubled breast. I've stirred up a hornet's nest over the port and must now work my way into the good graces of the ladies since the gentlemen have deemed me a latter-day Chartist and rogue."

James' eyes twinkled as he berated himself and he steered Marianne, with accomplished ease, through the heavy

Victorian furniture of his in-laws' house. Occasional tables abounded, weighed down with photographs and figurines. The new century had begun but the Maltby's domestic taste was firmly in the old.

Marianne's performance drew a look of genuine surprise from James who tried to mime both halo and wings as she relinquished her seat at the piano to her hostess. Captain Dehan and the vet had clapped loudest of all even though they arrived last and with unsteady steps. Anne drew her friend over to where her husband had seated himself.

"I told you there were pleasures to be had in the country," she said, her hand on his sleeve and turning her face to his. "If Miss Graves will permit us, we will visit her at New Hall and walk the grounds. The stables will delight you, I am sure."

The Captain offered his seat to Marianne as the vet struggled to his feet.

"No, no," said Marianne, alarmed. "Do not disturb yourselves. I need to join my father. We're going soon. But I know that we're free tomorrow afternoon, Anne, and we would welcome you to tea and show you the Estate."

"Am I included in the invitation?" asked James, joining them.

"Of course," replied Marianne, catching sight of her father. "Papa will be pleased."

The vet settled back down, with a groan. "Now there's one I wouldn't mind disturbing myself for if I were younger." He turned to James, with sodden, barely-focussed eyes. "As pretty as a picture and her father's only child. You could do worse."

MASTER OF THE HORSE

The next day proved to be fine. John and Marianne had walked back from church together and had a light lunch before their guests arrived. Introductions were made and the decision taken to tour the gardens while the light was still good. The ground staff had been dragging fallen timber and garden debris to the paddock on the far side of the house in readiness for Guy Fawkes. Several bits of discarded furniture poked out from the pile: their colours vying with the red-gold leaves. On the very top, a velour chaise-longue with horse hair and flock spilling from its sides made a throne for the Guy. The sun was low in the sky and the wind had a harsh edge to it but the group were undeterred. James helped Marianne across a patch of wet ground and fell into step beside her.

"I understand your father farms locally as well as running the Estate. He must often be away on business?"

"Yes, but then he often takes me with him."

"Not in the depths of winter, I should hope. Even angels feel the cold!"

Marianne shook her head and smiled in protest but she was saved from comment by her father asking her to lead the way to the orangery so that he could close the gates behind them.

The gardens were walked in proper fashion, with James making up for his brother's lack of questions and Anne finding everything delightful. The height of the tour was to be the stables and keen to show Anne her pony, Marianne went on ahead. Sage snickered as they approached. Gathering her skirts above the bedding, Marianne entered the stall. Addressing Sage in French, she slid her hand along the pony's mane, kissing her neck and softly stroking her silken nose.

"I think your pony stands in danger of being petted to death," smiled Anne.

"It's true, she is my consolation and my joy. Who else would put up with my nonsense? My father loves me dearly but is English to a fault and my great aunt Isabelle has lectured poor Tante Jeanne into believing that affection undermines morality. I envy you, Anne, both your mother's sweetness: and your husband's care."

"I knew you would have seen it!" said Anne, reaching out for Marianne's hand. "My husband is the kindest man alive and yet my parents wonder at my choice. It's hard for him – trapped inside his deafness – and defending me from his disappointed family who had hoped for an heiress at the very least." Marianne moved back to Anne's side and slipped her arm round her waist. "He was engaged before, you see …….He… . " Fabrice coughed to announce his arrival, preventing further talk as they heard John calling out Marianne's name. In some confusion, Fabrice stepped back as the others re-joined them. Their party now included Lord Harry and the Frasiers. Lord Harry was in expansive mood. The Dehans shared his love of horses and he was excited to discover that their father was the well-known owner and trainer of a number of top racing thoroughbreds.

"Miss Marianne, I do beg your pardon" he said. "I have not performed my introductions as I should. Lady Frasier, Miss Frasier – Marianne Robinson, whom you know and Mrs Dehan – Dr Maltby's daughter and Captain Dehan's wife." Lord Harry looked around to confirm he had completed the formalities and Sophia stepped to one side to reveal Fabrice, who had been making his escape.

"You have forgotten Monsieur Dupres, Lord Wellesden,

so I must make the introductions myself – May I introduce you all to my Master of the Horse!"

Fabrice nodded but did not speak and Lord Harry scowled. No one stepped forward to shake hands and Fabrice turned his attention to Sage, with grave deliberation. Sophia looked around in ingenuous triumph, enjoying the tension she had caused but the socially gifted James stepped into the breach.

"If Miss Frasier has a Master of the Horse, it is to be presumed she is a mistress of the equestrian arts herself. Should we therefore expect to see you at the hunt, tomorrow?"

"I doubt that very much indeed, my sister is a fair-weather rider," said Portia, "but you will see me! I've had my hunter sent down from home and it's his first time out this season."

James had broken the silence but not the tension. The Misses Frasier began a hissed recrimination between themselves as the party moved out into the chill evening air and Fabrice exchanged a mortified look with Marianne before she followed after them.

THE HUNT

The first of the month was a regular hunting day at New Hall with friends of the family and local farmers taking part. Lord Harry was expecting several visitors from London and the indisposition of one of this group had enabled Captain Dehan to take part. Dress was informal with hacking jackets being more the order of the day than pink but even so, the sights and sounds broke enticingly through the morning mist and a fair-sized crowd had gathered in the stable yard to see them off.

Anne and Marianne stood either side of Lady Wellesden just inside the archway and safe from the increasingly excited horses. The hounds had been brought round; their supple bodies intertwining like shoals of fish and their bell-like voices adding to the general hubbub. Lord Harry, with Lady Frasier at his side, saluted his grandfather and led the hunt out through the arch as the whippers-in marshalled the hounds. Captain Dehan and his wife exchanged a look of tenderness and the hunting party jostled through the archway and away over the home pasture. The younger Miss Frasier, who was dressed in riding attire that would not disgrace Hyde Park, had chosen not to ride. She was perched precariously on a mounting block to wave to her sister, with James Dehan in slightly anxious attendance.

"My brother-in-law declares himself totally smitten," said Anne, once the friends had relinquished Lady Wellesden into the care of her maid.

"But they have only just met," exclaimed Marianne, glancing in Sophia's direction as she leaned on James' shoulder to get down from the block.

"Not Miss Frasier, you precious goose. He means you! His 'dark angel'."

Marianne laughed out loud and widened her eyes. "I don't think I'll let his protestations turn my head yet awhile. Your brother-in-law is charm personified and therefore welcome in any company but he is 'pas sérieux' as the French say."

"You may be proved wrong. He is under family orders to adopt a more dignified lifestyle and foster his career – there are hopes of a political future as I understand it."

"And you think a half-breed, country mouse would be the answer, do you?"

"Certainly not! ……. But you might be, Miss Mouse ……."

FIREWORKS

Portia excused herself to Lady Wellesden and took her sister's arm, moving away from the warmth of the bonfire.

"Where have you been, you wretch? I've been stuck with my future mother-in-law this last half hour. She is a fount of wisdom on all things musical but really not my idea of a stimulating companion."

Sophia looked back towards the fire-lit scene. The family from the Hall were seated on a dais, their garden chairs festooned with lustrous wraps and travel rugs to keep out the chill. The Estate children were crowded round the toffee apple stand that cook had provided and were being roughly bossed about by older brothers and sisters. Each time the fire dropped and crackled, the children roared an echo; their voices raising skywards with the sparks.

Sophia's gaze stiffened as the outline of a man was silhouetted by the fire, she then smiled and turned back to her sister.

"I went back to the house to get my shawl: I found I was getting cold."

"Well, you've missed a real treat: crazed locals dancing round the blaze like pagans. His Lordship lighting the ceremonial flame - All features of a New Hall Guy Fawkes that I am doomed to witness for the rest of my married life."

Sophia now looked at her sister in earnest.

"Are you really so unhappy? I thought you two got on well together?"

"Oh, in that respect, I have no complaints: we have reached an unstated agreement to mostly ignore each other. It's all this Lady of the Manor palaver. Lady Wellesden and I are actually going to visit the sick, tomorrow! Why would I want to visit the sick? I don't like to visit at the best of times! I would rather join you at your riding lessons. Riding astride cannot be more difficult than side saddle and you must be positively adept, with all this extra practice you have had."

Sophia quickly looked away and then replaced her scowl with a smile.

"I hardly think your fiancé would give his unstated agreement to that, sister dear! Much too harem scarem for his lady wife-to-be. Why don't I come with you on the sick visits in place of Lady Wellesden? We might even drive ourselves if we stay on the Estate. We can drop the charity parcels off as quick as you like and spend the rest of the morning out on the perimeter road seeing how the matched bays perform."

Portia managed a smile in return but looked unconvinced.

"Would you, Soph'? That's unusually good of you. In fact, much too good to be true. What do you want me to do for you?"

"Nothing," replied Sophia, tossing her head as if offended. "Not one thing. Just say 'yes' and we can go and join the others for the firework finale! You would not want to miss that now, would you?"

The fire had settled to a calm red centre but the air around was still warm and a wood-smoke haze hovered just below the tree-line. Fireworks had been placed in the nearby paddock and while all eyes were turned toward the scurrying figure of Jem, who was charged with lighting the fuses, James Dehan walked across the fire-lit circle to address Marianne. Having greeted Anne, her companion, he took Marianne's proffered hand in his, drew it to his chest and continued to hold it as he moved to stand beside her. Marianne withdrew her hand but not before her father had noted the warmth of Dehan's gesture. John had been in close conversation with Robert Baker but his shudder of annoyance drew Dehan's behaviour to Robert's attention too.

"There's something about that man," said John, uncharacteristically speaking his mind. "I can understand why he might admire my daughter but Marianne is not used to London ways. And there will be talk. She needs someone steady: not a popinjay who can charm the birds out of the trees. Someone who will look after her."

John twisted the fingers of his gloves and avoided Robert's eye:

"This last month or so, I've hardly seen her. She is rarely at home if I happen to return for lunch and she seems ill at ease when I ask her about her day. It is not that I don't trust her or that I want to keep her penned up at home. It's just - I don't know - it's not easy being a father when there is no mother to show the way. I'd like to see her settled. Close to home; where I can still take care of her."

Something about John's tone gave Robert cause for hope. Diffidently, Robert faced his friend and mentor.

"I have known your daughter since she was a girl and would never see her come to harm. She knows me as an older brother or a favourite uncle: she has spent time at my farm with my sisters when they were at home and they all love her dearly." Studying John's face for his clue to continue, Robert added.

"If I thought there was a chance that we could be more than old friends, I would be a truly happy man. I've built the farm up and I'm proud of what I've done but it has been at the cost of my home life - - and, lately, I've begun to realise that I've got the farm but I've no one to share it with - - and no-one to pass it on to .."

The squeal of the first rocket fractured the night air and the crowd pressed in towards the paddock rail. Their conversation interrupted, John and Robert looked back over towards Marianne as James Dehan, with an ostentatious show of gallantry, raised his cloak to shield her from a firework's trail of silver stars.

"I am beginning to think my daughter spends too much time alone. It's a good thing that her Aunt arrives shortly, to spend Christmas with us. They will have plenty to occupy themselves with at home, once she arrives. I think I will ask one of the lads to lend a hand with that pony of hers. She cannot be forever at the stables when her Aunt is here."

SECRETS

Fabrice was leading Sophia's Arab back into the stable when Marianne arrived.

"Is Miss Frasier not riding, today?" she asked, as Fabrice started taking the tack off.

"No. It seems not. Not today, not yesterday. Maybe she has had her fun. I saddle the horse up as instructed but I don't think I've seen her for a week or more. I see her around the stables: but not for lessons: not since before the fireworks, I think." He shook his head and stroked the horse's soft muzzle. "It's bad for the horse: not getting exercise: he gets more and more flighty. He needs to let off some steam. Maybe I will join you later on the well-behaved Sage? We could do some dressage – the boys are not joining us today."

"I'd like that. Will you ride the Arab?"

"Yes, it's better that he gets worked. I'll take him back to the ménage now and get some of the fizz out of him. How long will you be? Half an hour?"

Marianne settled down to the happiest part of her day as she groomed her little mare. She picked out her hooves and oiled them, then brushed her coat and combed out her mane. The once worm-eaten excuse for a pony was now gleaming with health and she chuntered with pleasure as Marianne shone up her top coat with a leather. Their companionship was interrupted by a sudden snicker from Sage, whose senses were sharper than those of his mistress.

Putting down the leather, Marianne could just hear a woman's voice, half laughing: half pleading, and the responses of a man as he playfully ordered silence. Placing the saddle on Sage's back, she smoothed the numnah and ran the girth up round the mare's belly. More yelps of laughter came from further back in the stable block and then footsteps approached. Sage whinnied as Sophia came into view. Dumbstruck at seeing Marianne, Sophia quickly looked behind her then collected herself, patting her hair into place and brushing her sleeves.

"Miss Marianne!" she exclaimed. "You startled me. I have just been for my riding lesson and was making my way back to the Hall. It is a nonsense that I have to maintain this secrecy just because of the convention about women's riding attire but I suppose there is no point in upsetting Mamma."

Sophia made as if to go but then turned back. "In consideration of Mamma, it would be for the best if you did not mention having seen me here today. She would be as appalled as your father, I think? This could be our joint secret, could it not?"

Without waiting for a response, Sophia left the stable. Marianne was annoyed by Sophia's implied threat and also somewhat bewildered. Her confusion was not lessened when she arrived at the ménage to find Fabrice engaged in practising flying changes on the Arab: a picture of determined concentration. Fabrice brought the Arab round to her: both man and horse were panting.

"I think I must be getting old," laughed Fabrice. "He's as keen as ever and I'm exhausted. It's a good job Miss Frasier did not have her lesson today: I think she might have got more than she bargained for. The horse was totally over-excited at being ridden after all this time. We have had rears and bucks just like the wild west. It's only just now that he's started listening to me."

Marianne said nothing and led Sage into the ménage: jumping up into the saddle with ease. She only had a short time to spare but she knew she would be placed on her mettle for every minute of that time.

John had initially wandered over to the stable with the intention of talking to Peter Robinson about someone lending a hand with Sage during Tante Jeanne's visit but he was told that the Head Stableman had gone into the village to negotiate for winter straw and John did not want to approach anyone without Peter's agreement. Marianne had set out for the stables, mid-morning, after spending time with Lady Wellesden, and he expected her back for lunch. Leaving the main yard as the old clock chimed twelve, John decided to seek his daughter out so that they could walk back together. Sage was stabled with the other ponies and the work horses, in a block tucked behind the barn that the hands used as an indoor ménage in the winter months. Turning into the pony block, John practically stumbled into James Dehan who was scurrying, head-down, out of the side entrance.

"Mr Dehan!" he stated, interrogatively. "I thought this block only housed the working horses: not the thoroughbreds that interest you?"

James Dehan looked uncomfortably startled but he quickly recovered and put out his hand to John.

"Ah, yes. Just cutting through from the ménage. I've been speaking with Mr Robinson about those self-same thoroughbreds – one of them in particular, in fact. We are hoping to put her to stud at my father's yard. Robinson just needed more detail."

"So Mr Robinson is in the ménage? Good. I have been looking for him myself."

"Well, certainly, he was a moment ago. Although he was suggesting that he needed to attend to another matter before lunch so he may well have left by now."

John looked James full in the face and held his gaze before James once again proffered his hand and left.

John approached Sage's stall, breathless with anxiety. The pony stood contentedly, still saddled but with the stirrups run up and the bridle tied in a knot. His daughter was nowhere to be seen. The door belonging to the small feed store in the centre of the block creaked and Marianne emerged, adjusting her petticoats and fastening the last of the train of small buttons running up her sleeves. John's head filled with blood and his eyes stared. His snarl of anger merged with a moan of despair and his cry of "Marianne," sounded like the last plea of a drowning man. Appalled, Marianne ran to his side.

"Papa, papa, what is the matter? You are ill!! Let me help you. Papa, papa, look at me!"

John was slumped against the side of the stall and clutching at his collar, his face suffused with colour and chin trembling with emotion.

"So that's where you have been? I fondly believed your stories of Sage, your time with Sage, your delight in Sage! While all this time you were – and with him, Marianne. A vain, pretentious man: a man not worthy of you."

In the face of Marianne's amazement, John swung round as if to punch the wall and Sage skittered sideways. "Well, Miss, there will be no more excuses that feature Sage. . . may Sage. . be damned. You will not see Sage again. You will not return to the stables again. You will not move out of my sight again."

John barely contained a sob and Marianne tried to comfort him but he pushed her back.

"But Papa, it was to be a surprise for you. I knew you would worry but I thought that if you saw me when I had gained my confidence. . I promise, .I have been safe. I've been safe at all times."

John was barely registering his daughter's words. The image of her emerging from the feed-store in a state of relative undress blotted his vision and closed his ears.

"That villain," he growled, his eyes starting out of his head. "You think that he has a mind to your safety? To your reputation: to your good name? How could you be so foolish as to meet like this in secret? Such deceit! What kind of man would encourage such a thing?"

"But it was I who asked Monsieur Dupres. He was not part of the secret. He just let me join in with Mr Robinson's boys . . . ."

As if in response to his name, Peter Robinson entered the stables through the main doors. Both father and daughter looked around frantically as he stood outlined against the light. With an immense effort of will, John steered Marianne to the back of the stall at the far side of Sage.

The Head Stableman called from the door: "Mr Graves, are you here? It's Peter Robinson. I heard you were looking for me."

John came out of the stall, desperately gaining his equanimity. In a strangely thick voice, he responded to Peter's call.

"Robinson, there you are. I understand you've been in the village?"

Before leaving, John rasped at Marianne:

"You, you can just make yourself decent and then meet me back at home. Do not, I repeat, do not leave until I have spoken with Mr Robinson and do not let anyone see you in this state." He turned his back on her and called out:

"No need to join us, Robinson, I'll come back with you to the main block. It's my daughter's pony that I wanted to speak about."

Marianne crouched in the back of the stable, sobbing silently. Sage nibbled the top of her head, shuffling from side to side as if deciding what to do. Hearing someone approaching, Marianne lay further back into the straw but Fabrice quickly realised she was there. Pushing Sage gently to one side, he dropped down to his knees.

"Mademoiselle!" he cried, peering round her trembling fingers into her tear-stained face. "What has happened? What is the matter? Tell me, are you hurt? I will get help . . ."

"No, stop!" blurted Marianne.

"Stop!" she pleaded, now sobbing more loudly and twisting her head from side to side in a tortured grimace.

Fabrice reached out and gripped her shoulder as she

began to slowly bang her head against the rough wooden walls of the stall. She looked down at his hand as if surprised to find him there but stopped her wretched rocking and clamped her lower lip between her teeth. With a heaving intake of breath, she clutched her upper arms, her knuckles white with the tension of holding herself so tightly. Fabrice remained silent with his head bowed. Slowly, Marianne released her arms and brought her hands down to her lap.

"My father has taken Sage away. I can never see her again." Her voice tailed off as she mournfully gazed at the pony.

"But why? Why would he do that? You must be mistaken."

"No, no. He must have found out about the riding. He came into the stables as I was changing back out of my riding breeches. He says I've ruined my reputation and our family name. He forbids me to ever see Sage again."

Fabrice rested back on his heels, shaking his head as Marianne unthinkingly wiped her face on her sleeve.

"You must be wrong. Your family name besmirched because of riding: the ladies at the Hall ride every day . . . ."

"No, you don't understand. I now think he never wanted me to ride, under any circumstances. But he was so proud of my mother and he will not let anyone touch the photographs of her on horseback. I thought that if I rode well, I could surprise him and he would be proud of me too. But, how could he be when it was a horse that killed my mother?"

Marianne began to wail again, dashing the tears from her eyes with the back of her hand.

"I want my mother," she cried, opening her arms out towards Fabrice.

He gently drew her up and rested her head against his chest, her body heaving with sobs as she sank into near-hysteria.

"Be calm. There, there. Be calm," he whispered, gently rocking her in his arms. "Be calm. There must still be some mistake."

Marianne struggled in his arms and twisted her face to his. Tear-sodden and trembling, she wrenched at her hair where it had fallen across her face.

"I think, he thinks that I will be killed too – like her – You didn't see him. I've never seen him like that. He was beside himself. He despairs at my deceiving him and – and I did deceive him. I deceived him because of my stupid need to show him how clever I am: how like my mother I am. I deceived a man who has not one deceitful bone in his body, who finds deceit despicable."

Marianne now gripped at Fabrice in terror.

"He will send me away – where will I go? He will, he will send me away. He must despise me so. I know how much he wants me to behave like a young woman he could be proud of and yet I spend my time riding around on ponies like one of the farm boys." Marianne thrashed her way out of his arms and made as if to leave.

Grabbing her arm, Fabrice spoke slowly and calmly.

"No. Stay still. No one must see you like this. Your father would not wish anyone to see you like this."

Fabrice's tone of authority when added to her father's departing wishes broke through Marianne's determination and as if at the pull of a switch, she collapsed against the side of the stall. Her colour drained and Fabrice laid her gently back down among the bedding. She awoke with Fabrice wetting her temples and wrists with his scarf that he had plunged into Sage's water bucket. Sage herself had moved alongside like a brood mare guarding her foal. Marianne pushed up on her hands but Fabrice restrained her. She took the scarf from him and wiped the whole of her face and neck, shivering with the impact of the ice-cold water.

"I must go," she said, once again pushing herself to her feet. Her eyes looked sunken in her pallid face. "You will feed and groom Sage for me?" she asked, her lips twisting with the effort of holding back her tears. Fabrice moved back to her side and with unthinking tenderness slid his arm around her shoulders. Marianne leaned into his protective arm for the space of one long sigh and then turned to shake his hand. As if in explanation, she confided:

"I do remember my mother, you know. I remember her holding me, I think. Wrapping me in a warm towel after my bath and singing to me as I went to sleep. I try to think about her every night so that those pictures will not fade. I hoped that my father would one day love me as she always did but . . ."

Fabrice dropped her hand almost peevishly and stepped back, fixing her with his spirited gaze.

"I think you must have had to be brave when your mother died and now you must be brave again. I think that when your father knows that you were safe, he will forgive a few improprieties of dress."

The stable clock sounded the half hour. Fabrice removed the straw from Marianne's hair.

"Leave now before Jem comes to put Sage out in the paddock. Go by the side door, through the tack room. And be brave!"

Marianne slipped back into her sitting room while her father was at lunch. Unable to face him, she told their maid, Amy, that she was not hungry when she knocked at the door to ask if Marianne had eaten. Her teeth were chattering though her head was hot and as she fell into a fitful sleep her dreams were of her mother but her mother in riding attire smilingly riding alongside Fabrice. Then she and Fabrice were on horseback together, with his arm around her waist as they cantered through the woodland near Tante Jeanne's farm in France. She could smell the long sun-filled grass and felt calm and carefree. The horse moved beneath with effortless speed.

She woke to the drumming of hoofs that gradually migrated into a hammering at their front door. It was dark and her cheeks had dried tight with tears. She was still clutching the scarf. It smelled of molasses and honey- straw and the gipsy himself. Holding it to her face, she nestled into it, drawing her knees into the armchair and shivering with cold. Her father must be home and yet he had not been to see her. He could not bear to see her. Looking at the ashes in her grate, her eyes began to fill with tears again. She could hear raised voices in the hallway, the sound ebbing and flowing and then falling into less heated conversation. The voices stopped and the bang of the outer door sounded the visitor's departure. Stiff with cold, Marianne edged out of the chair and went to the doorway: only to stumble back again as footsteps came along the corridor. There was a knock and her father entered.

"Marianne?" he asked in a tremulous tone: unable to make her out in the winter gloom.

Marianne moved forward at the sound of his voice. His anger seemed to have disappeared but his voice betrayed uncertainty and wretchedness.

"I am here, Papa. I have not dared to come to you. I know you cannot forgive me"

John leaned forward and took her hand.

"No, no, it is I who should ask forgiveness. My suspicions were unworthy. I just wish you had told me. Surely I am not such an ogre that you had to hide your wish to emulate your mother from me?"

John's voice trembled and the depth of his emotion; normally held in such firm check, brought the tears back into Marianne's eyes.

"I just wanted you to love me, Papa."

"Oh but I do, Chou-chou. I do." In a rare moment of softness, John drew his daughter to him and held her, weeping, on his chest.

"No more secrets, Chou-chou. No more secrets and no more misunderstandings."

REJECTION

Marianne became feverish in the days following the discovery of her secret and the reconciliation with her father. Dr Maltby was called and his visit was quickly followed by one from Anne. She was ushered into Marianne's bedroom by Amy, whose abilities as a nurse had surprised everybody. Anne could have been attending a harvest festival from the amount of fruit she was carrying and enticing books and albums peeped out of the basket that Amy carried in her wake. While recognising that she had been unwell (to the point of overwhelming concern on the part of her father) Marianne was now beginning to feel a fraud. She was desperate to go back to the stables and desperate to confide in someone.

Anne was also full of news and was relieved to find her friend out of bed and sitting at the fireside.

"I am so pleased that I was able to see you before we have to leave. My husband has business in town so I will go with him and James has already returned to his chambers but not without sending his 'affectionate' wishes for his dark angel's speedy recovery."

Marianne brushed this comment aside with a wave of her hand and settled her friend next to her.

"You may thank your brother-in-law for his good wishes but there is someone else for whom I have a far greater debt of gratitude. Just before I became ill, my father discovered that I had been having secret riding lessons and he was furious. I had been banned from the stables: banned from Sage: banned from leaving the house. And then, somehow, he was persuaded out of his fury. Apparently, Monsieur Dupres marched into the house, stood his ground with my father and made it right. He must have convinced Papa that I was in no danger and that deceiving him had been very far from my intention."

"Dark angel, indeed!" retorted her friend. "Dark horse, more like. What were you thinking of, deceiving you father in such a way?"

"And I don't suppose you have ever done any such thing, have you?" Marianne retorted, her blush giving her cheeks an even healthier glow.

It took two more days before John let his daughter outdoors and then she was swaddled like a baby. Her first visit was to the stables in search of Fabrice. As she approached, her chest felt tight and her breathing became shallow. She was desperate to thank him for intervening with her father and felt a thrill of expectation but also of trepidation at seeing him again after he had comforted her and entered into her dreams. She was denied the straightforward meeting that she intended, however, since she found Fabrice in the company of Lord Harry Wellesden. Her arrival appeared to cause consternation for Lord Harry. He barely acknowledged her and looked highly displeased with the interruption. Put off her stride, Marianne's words of thanks somehow disappeared off her tongue and instead she found herself upbraiding Fabrice.

"I'm not surprised you have not been to visit me while I have been ill now that you are in such demand from his Lordship," she began.

"You have been ill?" responded Fabrice, fixing Marianne with an anxious gaze.

"With Miss Frasier and his Lordship to attend to, I doubt you will have time for Sage or our lessons now?"

"What has been the matter? I did not know that you had been ill."

Marianne tutted, waving away his concern, in seeming exasperation. "Oh - the illness is neither here nor there. The point is that my aunt will arrive shortly to spend Christmas with us and I will not be able to come to the stables as often. I had hoped that, this being so, you might teach me to ride side-saddle so that I can, at least, show my father that I have not been wasting my time. I could even ride outside the school: and without offending anyone if I ride like a lady." Marianne turned her head away from Fabrice's bewildered look and pursed her lips in annoyance.

"You seem angry with me, Mademoiselle, and you tell me you have been ill. Please tell me that you are now better. I would be wretched if I thought you had come to any harm because of the riding." He moved closer and tried to face her. His look of concern and hurt needed no words and Marianne blushed. Pulling his scarf out from her coat, she held it out to him, her eyes downcast.

"I – Forgive me, this is not what I came to say," she stammered. "Of course I am not angry with you. I . ." She proffered the scarf again and Fabrice took hold of it, finally looking full into her face.

"Ahh, there you are, Dupres!" said Sophia, with a swish of her whip. "I was expecting you in the school. No horse: no lesson! What has happened? It is unlike you to disappoint me. I thought I was your favourite pupil!"

Fabrice turned a completely blank face to Sophia as she arched an eyebrow in Marianne's direction. Twisting the scarf around his wrist, he declared, in his increasingly excellent English: "I will bring the Arab to the school, Miss Frasier."

Sophia watched him leave. "I think my Master of Horse begins to give himself airs! Or perhaps the poor young man is suffering. He treats me with such disdain and yet his eyes follow me everywhere. I imagine he meets very few ladies and it is clear that he does not know how to behave towards them."

Marianne physically backed away from this unsolicited

and quite improper conversation but Sophia had not finished there.

"I hear that he has refused to ride for Lord Wellesden in the point-to-point. He declares that he will only ride for himself! My future brother will not like that for an answer: he needs some gipsy luck to get him out of the horse-racing doldrums. Never mind. Once I have teased Monsieur Dupres back into humour with me, I will try my best wiles on his Lordship's behalf. His Lordship's father has returned from Germany. Lord Wellesden Senior runs a tight ship and will want a clear account of his firstborn's progress during the months he has been away. Gipsy luck will definitely be needed."

Sophia looked closely at Marianne for her reaction and discerned a glimmer of something that appeared to make her think her words had been worthwhile.

"I had better not keep my poor, lovelorn Master of Horse waiting one moment longer," she declared.

"Monsieur Dupres," she called, her voice filled with suppressed laughter as she emphasised his title in mock deference. Marianne's face turned deathly white, with just one feverish spot on either cheek. Her heart pounded but she did not feel ill. She was standing stock still and tense, listening for a man's reply: remembering similar laughter from the day her father discovered her in the stables.

CHRISTMAS AT NEW HALL

With Tante Jeanne arriving shortly, the preparations for Christmas were taking up the greater part of Marianne's time. Her mornings were spent with Lady Wellesden, who took personal interest in arrangements at the Hall, and her afternoons were spent in ensuring that everything would run smoothly at home. She had visited Robert Graves' farm, to collect the Christmas food they had on order and had a happy re-meeting with his sisters, who had returned for the holidays with their various offspring. Marianne had always been a favourite with them and their fondness seemed undiminished. The highlight of her visit had been an improvised treasure hunt when they went egg-collecting in the barn, with the children and a surprisingly high-spirited Robert in tow.

Following the lead of the late Queen, the Graves' had brought a fir tree into the house and Marianne had dressed it with bows and tiny candles. Each candle sat in a silver metal holder that clipped onto the tree's frond and when lit, their honeyed fragrance mingled with the pungent smell of pine. Glossy-leaved ivy, entwined with holly, ran across the beams and bunches of mistletoe adorned the hallway. Amy had helped make trains of golden paper stars that hung in cascades from the picture rail and pomades of cloves nestled among the bowls of nuts and candied fruit that festooned the sideboards.

Tante Jeanne had arrived a few days before Christmas

along with a scurry of light snow and had been bustled into Marianne's sitting room to recover while John organised the transfer of her valise. Pinched-looking from the journey, her Aunt's face brightened into wreaths of smiles as she clasped Marianne to her and Marianne had tears in her eyes as she held her Aunt's tiny hand and noticed, for the first time, her greying hair. Tante Jeanne, the scatty but determined Tante Jeanne, for whom nothing was a problem, looked vulnerable and lost and Marianne's response combined a sense of shock, concern and something close to irritation that her Aunt should prove not to be invincible.

By Christmas Eve, her Aunt had totally recovered from the journey, however, and their relationship had gone back to where it left off: her Aunt stringently supervising Marianne's time at the piano as she practised a piece to be played at the Hall. With all the activity, Marianne had barely been to the stable and had not seen Fabrice. Jem had remarked that Fabrice was back in France and the news had made her catch her breath until she realised he was there on business and was coming back. She suffered the same disturbing effect when she spotted him in church on Christmas morning. Happily, he was sitting well behind her and she could fix her full attention on the lessons and carols, behaving with such immaculate propriety that she received a pat on the hand and a nod of approval from Tante Jeanne.

The Estate church was full to overflowing with both staff and their visitors. The lessons were delivered by members of the Duke's family and it was particularly gratifying for Marianne to see the care that the Marquess, Lord Wellesden, was extending to his wife. Lady Wellesden's sight had continued to get worse, as had been predicted by her doctors, and she took her husband's arm out of need as well as courtesy.

The church had been built shortly after New Hall itself. Small but with ornate wooden carving, the building was encircled in fine old yew trees and very little of the low winter sun came through the stained glass windows. Candles had been placed in the sconces and each pew was decorated with greenery and festive ribbon. In the kindly light, Lady Wellesden looked years younger than her actual age and her serenity as she listened to her husband read out the passage from Matthew's gospel gave her face an angelic gleam. On finishing the passage, the Marquess looked towards her and, as if feeling his eyes upon her, Lady Wellesden's face lit up in response. As the Duke's eldest son, the Marquess spent a great deal of time away from England attending to family business but it was clear that he still valued his time at home and his wife of thirty years.

Anne looked across to the Family pew: with the Duke; his son, the Marquess, and his grandson, Lord Harry Wellesden, sharing the same profile across three generations. The sense of history was almost palpable as the families of the Estate: from the highest to the lowest, celebrated the Christmas service together.

******

There were numerous friends in church. Anne had returned to the Maltbys and the Bakers were there, in force. With so many introductions to make, the Graves' progress out of church was slow. Marianne was particularly happy to properly introduce Anne's husband, Captain Dehan, to Lady Wellesden and noted how his usual stern expression melted away as he lent towards her to exchange greetings.

The Family from the Hall were leaving for London the day after Boxing Day and staying away for the New Year. Their visit was being hosted by Baron Glamorgan, an elderly relative of the Frasiers who would be giving Portia away at her wedding to Lord Wellesden, in the spring. Miss Frasier's father had died when she was quite young and she had spent a great deal of her childhood with the Baron's family, joining him on the hunting field and on his foreign travels. It was rumoured that she would inherit his considerable wealth to add to that bequeathed to her by her father and the Baron was certainly being very fatherly with regard to his wedding duties; insisting that the young couple stay in town to finalise arrangements and providing his semi-adopted daughter with a trousseau fit for a Queen.

Marianne had learned of the Family's plans from Lady Wellesden who would be returning to New Hall shortly after New Year with her father-in-law, the Duke. Both she and he loved the London season of opera and soirees but they also found that a full diary of events took its toll on their health. Marianne promised to visit Lady Wellesden before she left and made her way out to the porch amongst the very last of the churchgoers. She was surprised and unnerved to find Fabrice hovering in the porch, therefore. He greeted her politely but his real show of warmth was for Tante Jeanne. He bent over her hand, in an old-fashioned salute, and she returned his greetings in voluble French: seemingly delighted by his courtesies.

As they walked back, Marianne could not resist enquiring about their exchange:

"I did not know that you had met Monsieur Dupres?"

"And that is because you did not stop to think how I managed to travel from France on my own! Do you think that your father would have left me to travel alone? No, of course not. The gallant Monsieur Dupres escorted me during the whole journey. He could not have been more attentive. Such charming manners. The Brothers have obviously completed the work started by Le Comte. He was his protégée, you know? Perhaps more than that? The nobility has never lived according to prevailing moral values. And Monsieur Dupres, he has a certain air . . ."

"Tante Jeanne!" exclaimed Marianne.

Her Aunt raised an eyebrow, re-asserting her authority. "Do not pretend to be shocked. These things are only to be expected of the aristocracy. They do not behave as we do and one can hardly blame poor Monsieur Dupres . . . His propriety goes without saying, having been raised by the

Brothers. He was intended for the Church, you know, and, although he seems to have found another life, he was full of praise for the Brothers and the education they gave him."

Marianne bit her tongue as the words: "but he's a gipsy!" were on the verge of spilling out.

"I can see you are shocked. It is true that I have never been a monarchist but the French nobility have as long a history as your English Lords and the Church of France has never capitulated to the State over some King's outrageous infidelities. We French have a lot to be thankful for and you must not forget that, with your English ways and your time spent away from us."

Marianne squeezed her Aunt's arm as they re-entered the house and wished her Happy Christmas, with a kiss on both cheeks.

******

Boxing Day was their traditional day for opening gifts: and giving them. The Graves had bought Amy the most beautiful fitted coat and matching hat and she went off to see her parents, with dimples in her cheeks and the hat seated jauntily on her head. John had bought his daughter a side-saddle and was dazzled by her pleasure at receiving it. Tante Jeanne had assured her niece's suitability of dress by presenting her with an elegant but decorous evening gown in deep pink satin, with just the mere suggestion of a bustle and a cascade of same-material roses flowing down the front. Much less tightly-waisted than the early Edwardian style, it needed far less inhibiting corsetry and was noticeably less full in the skirt. Marianne was determined to wear it that evening, if only for its relative comfort: even though its lines were at the forefront of prevailing English fashion. Tante Jeanne also handed her a tiny leather-bound box with an unmistakable French feel. Overwhelmed by her Aunt's generosity, Marianne was close to tears when the silken lining uncovered an exquisite silver brooch in the shape of a rearing horse. The movement had been captured, exactly, interpreted by bold lines, uncluttered with further decoration. She gasped with delight and was about to embrace her Aunt again when Tante Jeanne confused her by asking to see the piece of jewellery that her niece had ordered from France.

"It is not really to my taste," Jeanne decided, having examined the horse minutely. "I am surprised that you commissioned such a piece but your father tells me that you have as strong a feeling for horses as your dear mother had. It was good of Monsieur Dupres to bring it back to England for you. Even though it is so plain, it demonstrates French craftsmanship. I don't suppose you could have found that in England, if you had tried. He was most insistent that I hand it to you along with your gifts. You look surprised? I imagine you did not think to receive it so soon. I do not suppose that it would have arrived until the New Year had he not acted as courier?"

Marianne took the brooch back from her Aunt's extended hand and blushed as she handed it to her father for his inspection.

The Marquess, Lord Wellesden, had uncovered his Christmas present to himself earlier in the day and had amazed the staff by driving around the Estate in a gleaming new automobile, shipped in from Germany. The Marquess already owned a motor vehicle but the staff had never seen anything like this wire-wheeled beauty. It had been built for racing and the Duke's son was determined to return to Europe and enter her in the Paris-Bordeaux road race. His arrival to see off the Hunt and join in the traditional stirrup cup had drawn as many eyes as the pink coats of the riders and he was at the centre of an all-male group, extolling the automobile's virtues, when the Graves arrived at New Hall for the Musical Soiree. All the senior New Hall staff were present as well as the Family. The music room was garlanded with greenery and candle-lit for the occasion. The punchbowl glimmered in the centre of the room and, as Lady Wellesden escorted Marianne to the piano, the soft light caught the glint of the younger woman's silver horse-shaped brooch; her one ornament, pinned to the shoulder of her rose-pink dress.

Lady Wellesden had already presented Marianne with a beautifully bound copy of "Chansons de France", printed on vellum and with the title etched in gold on red leather. Their earlier meeting had been to say goodbye since the Family were leaving for London straight after the point-to-point, which was to be held on the following day. They had spoken of Marianne's return to health and Marianne had been surprised by Lady Wellesden's assumption that Anne would be having a child in the New Year. Marianne herself had noticed that her friend had been looking both wan but strangely beatific when they had met in church but she knew that Lady Wellesden's sight was not acute enough to note this visual nuance.

"I see with more than my eyes," Lady Wellesden explained. "It was your friend's tone of voice, there was a richness to it: a tenderness that was maternal in quality. I do hope I have not betrayed any secrets! I have always had this uncanny sense of people's state of health and since my eyesight has become poorer, my other senses seem to have compensated. Perhaps I will be proved wrong – although, in honesty, it would be the first time. Forgive me for being so open with you, Marianne: I rather presumed that you knew."

THE POINT-TO-POINT

Rumour had it that this year's point-to-point had attracted interest from outside the County, with runners and riders coming from as far afield as London. Carriages could be seen leaving the Hall for the finish point which was situated at the back of the Bakers' farm. The Marquess had been determined to drive there in the automobile and had set out before the carriages so as to give his latest acquisition an airing before the lanes became crowded.

The onlookers had divided into discrete groups; with the party from New Hall occupying the high ground while a fashionably dressed but rowdy group of younger men and women had placed themselves close to a notoriously dangerous ditch that had proved to be the most thrilling obstacle in previous years. One of their party had a post horn and the group were managing to scandalize the local youth by carousing in a manner that would have gained them a severe reprimand from their village elders if they had behaved in a similar manner.

Anne and her husband were the first to greet the Graves on their arrival. She had "forbidden" her husband to ride, she informed them, and Lord Wellesden had chosen to put his horse with a jockey brought down from Town, rather than be one of the "gentlemen riders" who contested the event.

"I understand that the mad money is on Monsieur Dupres," she whispered to Marianne. "My brother-in-law has even persuaded my husband to make a bet. The Frenchman's horse has caused quite a stir, recently, and they say he refused the offer of Lord Wellesden's horse and only bets on himself."

Anne directed Marianne to the "London party" by the ditch where she could just make out James Dehan standing up in the back of a charabanc.

"He has come all the way from London to see the race?" exclaimed Marianne. "He must be mad!"

"Oh, there's quite a crowd of them, apparently: and a great deal of money changing hands. It's a fast set he is moving in lately."

The post horn drew their attention to the race and they looked across the valley to the start-post on the Druid's Mound. The course was over three miles and at times the riders were obscured from view by trees or folds in the land. The final stretch rose up from the valley bottom after crossing a small but fast-flowing brook. The infamous ditch had been built as part of an attempt to stop the top soil from eroding and was cut deep into the steep hillside two hundred yards back from the finish line: in a bottleneck between a closely-planted enclosure and a fenced-off road, it presented real problems to the rider. The only approach was over a crumbling field wall and the combination of the land falling away as the rider cleared the wall and then rising up again to the side of the ditch presented both a physical and strategic challenge.

Horses and riders suddenly appeared across the skyline with one or two stragglers already finding the ground too taxing. Captain Dehan offered his field glasses to Marianne.

"It is difficult to tell from this distance but you should be able to spot Dupres' little mare: she's by far the runt of the bunch. I'm surprised he entered her over this distance, even though she has been doing so well for him."

Marianne aimed the glasses in the direction of the start, feeling momentarily giddy as she skimmed across fields and clouds and finally located the riders.

"They seem to be peeling off in different directions?" she said interrogatively. "Are they allowed to do that?"

Captain Dehan laughed. "That's part of the skill. There is no set course and the riders can play it safe or take extra chances to gain on the others. Just down from the Start, they can cut off a couple of hundred yards if they jump the hedges at Bakers Crossing rather than looking for an opening, for example."

"What does your husband mean about Monsieur Dupres doing so well?" Marianne whispered.

"Apparently, he's the talk of the County," replied Anne. "He now owns several horses and he rides on the flat and over hurdles. They say he bought Folie, the horse he is riding today, from the gipsies and that she was probably stolen in the first place. It's like a novel!"

Captain Dehan let out a gasp as the riders appeared fleetingly in a gap between woodland on the far side of the valley and hurtled down towards the brook. Three riders were now bunched close together; separated from a fourth by several yards; with the rest of the field now well behind. "No!" he cried, as the second horse stumbled, almost bringing down the third. The near collision allowed the lead rider to pull further ahead, crossing the brook at its narrowest point in one powerful bound. The fourth rider had caught up ground coming down the hillside and took the water at a bounce, with a deer-like spring into the middle of a wider stretch of water and a hop back out. The lead horse was making heavy weather of the soft ground in the valley bottom and gradually the fourth rider, on a much lighter horse, was closing the gap.

Captain Dehan turned to his wife:

"The Devil, he might just do it!"

Anne placed her hand on his arm and caught his eye, his poor hearing sometimes meant that he raised his voice more loudly than he should.

"But, it's Dupres!" he said, leaning down and lowering his tone.

The crowd near the ditch had become galvanised. Several had joined James Dehan, standing on the seats of the parked vehicle and the post horn was sounding out over the general hubbub. A hundred yards further up the hill, on the edge of the group from New Hall, Marianne could feel the excitement mount from both sides. Lord Wellesden had taken his hat off to shade his eyes against the winter sun and his father had joined the Duke's party to get a better view. In the lead was the jockey from London, riding Lord Wellesden's hurdler, Wellington, but appearing from behind the enclosure was the little mare, ridden by Dupres.

The two horses approached the wall together with Wellington being spurred on to make the leap. The jockey had clearly decided to tackle the obstacle at one jump, intending to land at the far side of the ditch on the upward slope of the hillside. Meantime, Dupres checked the mare. Captain Dehan hissed in disappointment but there was no way that Folie had the stride to take the jump in one. Wellington plunged through the air, his powerful back legs pushing off from beneath the wall. His forelegs hammered into the hillside as the jockey brought him up-together but his offside hoof had clipped the edge of the ditch and the scree was falling backwards down the hillside. With a scrabbling movement, the horse tried to bring his rear legs forward, the jockey urging him on and brandishing his whip. Finally, with cheers from the crowd, Wellington righted himself and pushed on, up the incline and out of danger.

The drama of the leap had taken attention from the little mare. While Wellington struggled, she cat-jumped over the wall and teetered on the nearside edge of the ditch, momentarily loosening stones before taking off again to land delicately on the hillside. As the two horses reached the brow of the hill, Folie was in the lead. Dupres was riding without a saddle and now leaned forward, Indian-style. Wellington was gaining ground and the crowd was hysterical. Folie stretched out her neck as if running for a tape and, although some tried to protest and a fair few cursed, she won the race by a nose.

The crowd from the ditch viewing point came up to the finish line and the Duke of Newshire stepped forward to congratulate the winner. As the onlookers parted to make way for the Duke, the younger Miss Frasier appeared at his side, to his evident surprise. Monsieur Dupres dismounted and Jem threw a loose rug over Folie. Fabrice was wearing a tricolour over his shoulder and tied around his waist in ironic imitation of the silks worn by more professional riders. The Duke handed over the trophy, that was filled with guineas and went to look at Folie. The little mare instinctively drew back and tossed her head.

"Mr Robinson has told me that you had trouble with this one to start with, Monsieur Dupres. Some tale of warm water and an overhanging beam?"

Fabrice bowed before responding. "She came to me completely head-shy, your Grace. I could not even get a halter on her and she broke a rope every time she reared. Her owners had given up on her. The trick was to get her to rear under a bag of warm water hanging from a low beam. The water protected her head when she reared up but the impact burst the bag and the warm water ran down into her eyes and across her neck. It is supposed to make the horse think that it has injured itself and that blood is flowing out of a wound. Whether that is true or not, she can now be handled easily by a quiet rider but as you can see she is still full of spirit, as nimble as a goat and as brave as a lion."

The Duke smiled and patted Fabrice on the back.

"I must thank you most profoundly for allowing me to bring her to the Estates ménage when I was training her, your Grace."

"I think we were still in your debt for the effort you put into Hidalgo. He is the best prospect we have had at New Hall in years and with both Gloriana and Titania in foal by him we have a great deal to look forward to. I doubt if my son would agree with me, today, having seen his own horse beaten into second place, but we are all grateful to you for extending your stay with us."

Sophia had enjoyed the winner's limelight and now drew all eyes to herself by addressing Fabrice in mock command.

"Monsieur Dupres, your colours if you please! I always want to be on the winning side."

Fabrice looked at her with complete incomprehension.

"Your colours, Monsieur," she continued, pointing at the tricolour. "The courtly virtues first came from France and I have dubbed you my champion."

Grudgingly, Fabrice took the tricolour from his shoulder and handed it to Sophia. With a theatrical swirl, she wrapped it round the crown of her hat and looked to the Duke for applause.

"Most fetching," he responded, casting his eyes to the floor. "Do you wish me to escort you back to your friends? It looks as if the charabanc is about to depart."

"Oh, they will not leave without me," she replied.

"No, but the connecting train to London has no such sense of generosity. It would not do for you to miss it."

From the back of the crowd, Marianne watched Sophia accept Fabrice's colours and was forced to remember her earlier suspicions and Sophia's claim to be his "favourite pupil".

NEW YEAR: NEW BEGINNINGS

New Year without the Family would be strange but the Graves' chose to honour the occasion with a party of their own. John had taken over the upper rooms at the King Rufus, the closest hotel to the Estate, and had invited several families with whom New Hall did business as well as the Bakers and the Maltbys. The most senior staff from the Hall had also been invited and, out of courtesy to Tante Jeanne, so had Fabrice. The cold but bright weather of the Christmas period had turned wet and now the clouds were banked up ominously as the guests arrived.

Marianne opened the dancing with her father who handed her to Robert Baker when that dance came to a close. Knowing Robert did not dance, she was surprised to be offered his hand when a waltz was announced and even more surprised as he studiously counted his way round the floor, frowning with concentration but managing to avoid her toes. While dancing, she had caught sight of her Aunt sitting alone in an alcove and so excused herself to Robert and left the floor once the waltz ended.

Stooping to kiss her aunt she asked, "Are you content here on your own, Tante Jeanne? I am happy to sit with you."

"I am not here alone. Monsieur Dupres offered to find some refreshment for me and he should return at any minute."

Marianne blushed and then silently scolded herself.

Fabrice returned and offered his hand. "Mademoiselle," he said, with a slight pressure to her fingertips.

"Mais, Monsieur!" exclaimed Tante Jeanne, addressing Fabrice in French. "You have brought me an ice when I know that it will kill me if I so much as look at it. I am sure I have told you about my sensitive tooth."

"A thousand apologies," responded Fabrice, looking disconsolate. "I will return to the dining room immediately and find something more suitable."

"And I will go with you to make sure," said Marianne.

In the empty lobby, Marianne grabbed her chance and quickly turned to Fabrice.

"Monsieur Dupres, the brooch – it is lovely - but you must let me know what I owe you."

"Owe me? What do you mean? I owe you my life, my reputation! The brooch is a small thing." Fabrice glared maliciously at his boots. "It is a gift," he remonstrated, looking her full in the face.

"Oh, but I cannot accept such a gift. You have already given me so much by giving me Sage. You exaggerate when you say I saved your life. I would do the same for anybody."

Marianne, bridled as he jerked away from her, the colour rising in his cheeks.

In a broken Gipsy-French she could barely understand Fabrice confronted her.

"Very well, accept the gift from 'anybody' then – from Jem, from Nolly, from Mrs Grundy and all her pretty girls. Do not regard it as a thank you from me. It is a thank you from anybody, from everybody, from nobody: and I hope that you can find it in your heart to like it!"

Marianne reeled. She had obviously wounded his honour and did not dare chase after him to try and put it right. Taking the brooch from her pocket, she pinned it through the folds of the scarf that she had draped around the neckline of her dress. Perhaps he would accept this visual apology. As she hesitated, the lobby filled with others making their way to the dining room and Marianne was swept up into her duties as hostess but now her unsolicited memory of Sophia sporting Fabrice's colours became mingled with the many faces of Mrs Grundy's "pretty girls" and others who followed the gipsy with their eyes.

MONSIEUR LE COMTE

By the time the party ended, the snow was falling. Mr Graves had booked rooms at the hotel for his family and Tante Jeanne had gone gratefully to bed. Father and daughter were alone in the lounge as the staff tidied up around them and they were sharing a kindly joke about the number of times Robert Baker had taken Marianne onto the dance floor to demonstrate his new-found skill.

"He's a good man," said John, reflectively "and almost as fond of you as I am."

Marianne looked closely at her father, but his gaze was fixedly elsewhere. As she framed a question, they were interrupted by the hotel manager.

"Excuse me, sir. There is a Mr Dupres in the foyer, wanting to speak to your daughter." As he spoke, Fabrice came into the room, carrying several items of ladies' belongings. He bowed to both of them.

"I am afraid I have failed in my duties to your Aunt, Mademoiselle Graves, since she has left without her spectacles case, her shawl and her evening bag. It is fortunate I made one last check, I would not wish her to think that they are lost."

Marianne smiled, "If this is failure then I too have failed on more than one occasion. My Aunt seems to leave a trail of belongings wherever she goes."

Fabrice proffered the items but Marianne hesitated. "I don't believe the shawl is hers, in fact. I do not immediately recognise it and it is most unlike her to so feel the heat that she would remove her shawl."

John sighed in slight exasperation.

"I will go with Monsieur Dupres to Reception, Papa, and see if anyone has reported a loss. I am quite happy to see myself to my room. You go up."

John kissed his daughter on the forehead.

"Very well, Chou-chou, the staff will make sure that you have everything you need. Good night Mr Dupres. Good night, my dear."

The shawl was handed into the manager and Fabrice turned to go.

"Would you join me for a warm drink before I leave? The staff seem in no rush and some hotel guests are only just returning from their various engagements."

Marianne accepted graciously, unconsciously stroking the brooch.

"I need to apologise - Not about your Aunt's belongings," he added, as Marianne tried to protest. "My behaviour about the brooch was unforgivable. I behaved like a spoiled child. But, you see, I have so little to give and then to have my gift scorned."

"It wasn't scorned," Marianne replied softly.

"Perhaps you think I stole it like they think I stole my horse?"

Marianne smiled. "Well if it was stolen, all I can say is that you have very good taste."

There was a comfortable silence while the waiter brought a chocolate drink.

"I did used to steal – I used to steal to live. But I was saved by le Comte and by God."

Intrigued, Marianne merely opened her eyes wider as an indication for him to continue.

"I do not remember how I came to be with the gipsies because they made it very clear to me that I was not one of their own. It was also clear that I was useful to them, however. Small and wiry, I was their best cat burglar, sneaking in through windows and opening doors from the inside so that they could make away with their pickings - and with no blood-ties to make them worry if I got caught. But, of course, I did get caught: eventually. It is to my eternal gratitude that my captor was le Comte. He saw off the gang with his shotguns and with threats of the Police and tied me to a pulpit in the chapel."

Marianne raised an eyebrow. Entranced by the tale her chocolate stayed untouched and she hardly breathed in case he sensed an interruption and stopped.

"That is where God comes in. I would not have been caught but I felt bad about stealing the cross. The cross was the reason I had been posted in through the chapel window: my benefactor has little enough of his former wealth elsewhere in the chateau. Small and glimmering in the moonlight, the jewelled cross cast a long shadow down the aisle. I knew that I was meant to grab it and hand it back through the window but it just felt wrong. It was so beautiful I was in awe of it but, more than that, it belonged to God.

To cut a long story short, Monsieur le Comte decided not to hand me to the Police but to the Brothers and they undertook to teach me, in exchange for my total obedience and a good deal of hard work in their kitchen garden. I also paid my way by working in the stables at the chateau and remembered enough of my gipsy ways to make sure that Monsieur le Comte made some very good deals when horse-trading. I can never re-pay him and never meet the high standards set by the Brothers. But I could never have become an acolyte, the lure of the horses and the outdoors was always greater than my wish to follow that sacred path. The gipsy influence obviously extended beyond a smattering of the language."

Marianne's eyes had continued to stare as this story unfolded and she might have heard more had not the waiter come to clear their untouched drinks. Fabrice rose to go.

"I will forgive you if you will forgive me," she said. "I love the brooch even though I do not deserve it and, most importantly, I would never wish to offend you."

Fabrice took her hand and for a lingering moment it seemed as if he would kiss it but, as if on second thoughts, he released her, turned on his heel and left.

RETURN TO FRANCE

The news of Tante Isabelle's ill health arrived early in January. Tante Jeanne disguised her anxiety with bustling and ineffective attempts at packing while insisting that she needed no help. Marianne had been intending to return to France but she and her father were still in the process of deciding whether she was to return to the Tantes' house for the Spring – as she had done in the past - or whether New Hall would become her year-round home. The decision was taken to not make a long-term decision until she had a chance to report back the current state of affairs to her father and, with that in mind, Aunt and Niece set off within two days of receiving the news, with Monsieur Dupres escorting them both.

"Seventy-nine is not old," Tante Jeanne asserted for the hundredth time. "She is strong and, you know, the village of Saint Gervais is famed for the health and longevity of its inhabitants." She stared out to sea as they left the harbour; she was repeating the phrase like a mantra and not expecting a response. Marianne settled her into their cabin for the night crossing and returned to the Salon. Fabrice had organised a light meal and asked if he might join her.

"It must be strange for you to return to France so often – it must increase your homesickness?" prompted Marianne after they were settled at the table in an almost deserted dining room.

"In a way. But I managed to meet up with le Comte de

Gilles when I was here last."

Fabrice offered her more wine and then returned to staring fixedly at the label as a tense silence developed.

"It's interesting. I feel at ease speaking French again and heading back to Saint Gervais but, increasingly, I regard New Hall as my home."

"So you think you will return for good after this visit?" responded Fabrice, almost accusingly. Marianne looked into his face to see where the tone was coming from but he would not meet her gaze.

"I too must return to England. I cannot leave until I know whether I can succeed."

"It seems to me, you are succeeding very well. My father tells me you have even bought some grazing: from the same farmer who sold you his carriage horse."

Momentarily, Fabrice's face came alive and he let out a Gallic snort of derision.

"Carriage horse! No wonder the poor horse was uncontrollable. He only has two speeds: stop and bolt – but Espérance will make the finest steeplechaser, ever!"

"You've called him Hope? A fine name for a horse that the world had given up on."

Fabrice looked up at her from under his eyelids, lowered his voice and asked:

"And do I have hope? I must return to England if there is any chance, but if there is none, then I want to be as far away as possible."

Reading confusion in Marianne's face, he continued:

"You must know that I must follow my heart. If the woman of my dreams is in England, that is where I must be – even though, however close in miles to her I am, she may still be way beyond my reach."

The image of Sophia flooded into Marianne's mind: her knowing look as she roped Fabrice's racing colours round her hat, the uneasy meeting in the stable and Sophia's indirect threat that bound Marianne to secrecy about having seen her there.

Fabrice was looking at her with a white-hot intensity. Her own face suffused with colour as she realised a moment of unutterable jealousy. In retaliation, she found herself wishing that Sophia and Fabrice would stumble into a scandal of immense proportions as long as she did not have to know about it. But her better nature overcame her searing disappointment. She must warn him.

"I know you think that love will prevail but you do not know the English class system as I do. You have a special place at New Hall because of your skills and because you are French but - ultimately . . . ."

"You give me no hope – none at all?"

"Fabrice, she is not brave enough – I know you will hate me saying this about the woman you love but however much she loves you she will not leave Society. Even she must have sufficient sense of family to see that marriage to you would damage her sister's position. I know it sounds ridiculous, in this day and age, but it's horribly, horribly true."

"Sister?" he queried, turning to face her.

"Lady Frasier, the future Lady Wellesden. Her place in Society is assured - but a scandal, particularly at this time, would hurt not only her family but the Duke's."

Fabrice, forgetting himself, reached out and grasped her hand.

"Marianne, what are you thinking? What do I care for Lady Frasier or her sister! It is you, Marianne, it is you I dare to hope for!"

"But . . . I . . ." Marianne felt her heart lurch as the boat trembled an echo.

"I . . . ?" the colour rushed back into her face and unsolicited tears swirled in her eyes.

"Fabrice, I cannot speak about this now. I am here with my Aunt. My father is waiting for news. I . . ."

She realised she was not making sense and sighed. Fabrice looked down at her hand which was still held within his,

"But is there hope?" he asked.

Marianne smiled through her tears and gently drew her hand from his.

"I. . . . my father . . . . ," she stuttered before standing and fleeing the dining room.

FOXY

Lord Brandon had reappeared in London within months of his disgrace at New Hall. As the Duke had promised, no respectable house or club would receive him but his money ensured that he did not want for companions and, with luck that was suspicious in its consistency, he had increased his fortune despite the costs of his dissipated lifestyle.

In financial desperation, Lord Wellesden had finally sought out his former friend. He had first spotted him in a private box at the Opera. Caruso, the most celebrated singer of the day, was performing Carmen during a visit from the New York Metropolitan. Despite the glittering nature of the occasion, Lord Brandon had drawn attention away from the stage as much by his ill-timed applause and loud greetings to acquaintances as by his exotic attire. With the braided trousers of a matador and silk-lined cloak, Brandie drew all eyes - as did his companion: the most ravishingly beautiful woman, dressed in the vibrant colours of a gipsy, whose gaudy earrings and sparkling bangles caught the light from the stage each time she turned to speak to her escort.

Lord Wellesden would not approach Brandie in public but he had a good idea of where to find his former friend and, on the following day, they practically collided with one another outside Foxtons –"Bookmakers to the Gentry" – as the sign outside declared.

"Wellie!" exclaimed Lord Brandon. "Never expected to see you off the leash! I bet your dear old Pa don't know you are here – or the sermonising Duke – Damn his eyes!"

Lord Wellesden pretended not to hear the slight.

"What's a chap to do, Brandie? The old times are gone. I am to be married at the end of March – to Lady Portia Frasier."

Brandie guffawed. "I had heard the news, old chap. I think I would have gone for the little minx Sophia if I had had my choice."

"Well, there's the thing, Brandie. Choices, yes, choices." Lord Wellesden moved back into a doorway and tilted his hat at an angle as an automobile drew up.

"Expensive business, weddings: but life's pretty expensive too. I suppose you heard about my horse, Wellington, losing out to Dupres' little mare at our local meeting? Unbelievable! I knew his mare was fast over the flat but who would have thought she had that kind of stamina. And where in God's name did Dupres find her?"

"Heard about it! I lost money on it. That Froggy fellow owes me in more ways than one. He can go back where he came from and take his filthy gipsy ways with him."

"Well, we have a chance to try and make sure that he does just that. I have a little offer to make to you. It will make both of us a pot of money and your gipsy chap will get his comeuppance."

Brandie noticeably perked up and drew closer to his former friend.

"They say he is racing in the opening meeting at Woodbridge. None of the big boys will be there but there'll be money changing hands, you mark my word. Dupres' mare is still to be beaten, locally. There were big London punters present when she won the point-to-point and I think some of them will be tempted to try their luck down in the country again."

Lord Brandon licked a slime of spittle from the corner of his mouth:

"Like you, I'm keen to spread my bets as much as I can: The Classics are a good day out but I don't waste my money on them. Too many bounders in the game, like Foxy here. You can see from this place that he only plays to win. Wiliest rogue I ever met. He has his snout in every trough – if there is a penny to be turned.

But, hold on, if the mare is as fast as you say she is and the rest of the field is not up to national standard, she will just win as an odds-on favourite – and where's the money in that?"

"That is where I come in. I know how to ensure she loses. If you can find us a credible contender and a jockey whom you have used before, I will guarantee you a win: against the odds and in support of your grudge against Dupres. Believe me, I need a win as much as you want one, Brandie."

"I have to say, it's tempting. It's less to do with the money and more to do with that low-life gipsy, whose word seems to carry more weight than my own. We have a month or two to make the arrangements and to raise a little betting fever amongst those who will spread the tip on to others."

As they had been standing, the light had got worse and the cold wind had started to contain fine wisps of icy rain. As if noting the automobile for the first time, Brandie hailed the chauffeur. Drawing Lord Wellesden forward with him, he threw open the rear door.

"There's someone I want you to meet, old chap. I believe you were present when she joined me at the Opera?"

Lord Brandon's companion from the Opera leaned forward. She was dressed in the height of fashion and her eyes and lips gleamed in the lingering light. At close quarters, in spite of the make-up, her relative youth was still apparent: her thin neck rising out of the boa feathers that swirled about her shoulders.

"Miss Moira MacDonald - an up-and-coming actress – not quite the fame of Mrs Langtry but I am doing what I can to emulate our former Prince! Say 'Good Evening' to the nice gentleman, Moira. There, you see, Wellie – she likes you. And there are plenty more where she came from, if you take my meaning."

Lord Wellesden glanced over his shoulder and moved back from the automobile.

"May we give you a lift anywhere, old chap?" asked Lord Brandon, sarcastically, as Lord Wellesden protested the little distance and his preference for walking. "I knew you would not dare! No need to worry on my account. I know to give you a wide berth in polite company – Your grandfather has one too many influential friends for my liking."

LES JONQUILLES

The Aunts' house was just outside the village of Saint Gervais, set in a large walled garden. With the typical hipped roof of the region, it had formerly belonged to the Church and still had a more formidable air than the cottages roundabout. On arrival, Tante Jeanne had scurried into the house ahead of them as Fabrice organised the luggage. Marianne stood in the hallway, dazed with anxiety and by the myriad of memories that swelled over her. Straining to hear the voices from upstairs, she gave her hat and coat to Madame Grislot, a woman from the village, who helped out at the house.

"How is she?" she asked, looking closely at Madame Grislot's inscrutable face.

"Old and tired, Mademoiselle," she responded, with a taciturn finality.

Tante Jeanne called Marianne to join her upstairs. The faintly medicinal smell of the sick-room segued out into the familiar smells of the house. Tante Isabelle was sitting in her enormous panelled bed looking so alarmingly small that for one moment Marianne thought there had been some mistake. But her great-aunt's rarely-bestowed smile welcomed her into the room and, as Marianne bent to greet her, she was relieved to find that Aunt Isabelle's voice was strong and that, far from being propped up by the pillows that surrounded her, Isabelle was leaning forward in anticipation.

Her Great Aunt immediately took charge.

"Well, my dear Grandniece, so here you are! Looking grown-up and quite the fine lady. Visiting your father obviously agrees with you despite the vile English climate and detestable English food. But we have you back with us now. Back where you belong and we will soon put the apples back in your cheeks. Call Madame Grislot, Jeanne. We will have a little soup and a glass of wine to get the warmth back into your limbs and I have asked her to serve supper early. I will join you downstairs. I have been malingering in this bedroom for too long."

Jeanne started to protest but a stern look from Isabelle kept her silent.

"Well, get along," Isabelle commanded, "and ask Monsieur Dupres to join us. Your letters in which you mention him, Jeanne, have intrigued me. Having le Comte de Gilles as one's 'benefactor', shall we call it, that is intriguing in itself."

"Surely, she is not well enough to leave her bed?" asked Marianne as she left the room with Tante Jeanne.

"I totally agree with you. Madame Grislot tells me that the doctor has been every day. Apparently, it is her heart and she has had these blackouts or whatever they are for some months: before I left for England, in fact, so how she kept her ill health from me I will never know. The doctor contacted me because early last week, she was discovered collapsed at the gate; unable to move, her speech slurred and in obvious distress. Not that you would believe that, today. She seems her old self – and just as strong-willed as she ever was."

"I must get word to my father. Since she is improving, I think I should just stay a couple of days then return to England, collect my things and come back to spend the winter in France as I always used to do."

"That would do her more good than anything."

GREAT AUNT ISABELLE

Being with Fabrice in her Aunts' house left Marianne strangely breathless. His quiet courtesy to her aunts was delightful to witness and she had to suppress her smiles when she caught the two old ladies vying for his attention and, in Aunt Isabelle's case, being positively coquettish. Her Great Aunt did look desperately tired but she amazed Marianne with her dry wit and the knowledge of world affairs that she displayed at supper.

In despite of the good company, both travellers and invalid were pleased to retire to bed quite early. Fabrice had been given temporary accommodation in Great Uncle Grégoire's study: a room unused for such a purpose for the last thirty years. Aunt Isabelle's husband, Grégoire, had died not long into their, admittedly late, marriage. The house had belonged to his parents and he had stayed in the family home taking care of them until they died. His marriage to Aunt Isabelle, already considered an old maid by many in the village, had caused something of a family rift at the time since there had been other claimants to the property and the lines of inheritance had been interrupted by Uncle Grégoire taking a wife.

Aunt Jeanne and Marianne helped Isabelle into bed and gratefully went off to their own rooms; Marianne clambering into her ornately carved bed with its horsehair mattress that was almost as high as her waist. Madame Grislot had been staying overnight while Isabelle had been ill and before going up to her room on the top floor, she had placed hot-water bottles into each bed, wrapped around with a piece of flannel sheeting.

Marianne had expected sleep to come immediately she lay down but the effort of travel and the tensions of the day had left her mind whirring even though her body ached with tiredness. She listened to the old house creak and complain as it settled down for the night, lulled by the wave-like groaning of the pines outside her window. Images of the day came back to her: the shock of first seeing Isabelle again, Jeanne's "brave" face as she stopped herself from weeping and the unsettling moments when Fabrice came close or he caught her in his gaze.

It was barely dawn when Madame Grislot appeared at Marianne's bedside. A bleak winter light peeked through the shutters and Marianne could see her breath in the air as she struggled to sit up from among the goose-feather bolsters into which she had been snuggled. Madame Grislot moved back to the foot of the bed.

"I think you must come, Mademoiselle, and send Monsieur Dupres for the doctor. I went into your Great Aunt to set the fire and she did not stir. She is awake but only makes a moaning sound."

Marianne was out of bed and dressing as Madame Grislot spoke, pulling a shawl around her shoulders against the chill of the morning.

"Where is Aunt Jeanne?" she asked.

"I have left her sleeping. She will need her sleep, I think."

Marianne crept into Isabelle's room, feeling strangely ashamed at not asking permission. Her Great Aunt was lying on her back with barely a breath escaping her lips. Her whole face had shrunk into her eyes, which stared preternaturally bright from her parchment skin. Marianne kissed her forehead and the eyes pleaded with a desperate urgency as her Great Aunt once again began to moan. A sob of fear and sadness burst from Marianne as she looked to Madame Grislot for guidance.

"I will send Monsieur Dupres for the doctor. Will you stay here?" she asked.

The rough-hewn Madame Grislot moved closer to the bed and tenderly took Aunt Isabelle's hand.

"She is the same age as my mother – they were girls together. My mother spoke of Isabelle on the very day she died and your Great Aunt never forgot their early friendship. I know that it was Isabelle who kept me in shoes and clothes when we lost the farm: my brothers too. We do not forget such kindness."

Assured that her Great Aunt was in good hands, Marianne ran down the stairs. She tapped gently on the door to the study and waited. Careful not to raise her Aunt Jeanne just yet, she opened the door and entered. The light from the hallway fell across the chaise longue that Fabrice had used as his impromptu bed. Sensing her presence he stirred and swirled his head round to the light. Without prompting, he jumped to his feet, pulling the bed covers along with him.

"What is it?" he asked, with such concern in his face that Marianne delivered the message from across the room and then ran back to the sick room as a way of not running into his arms.

A DEATH, A FUNERAL AND A WILL

The doctor's arrival would have woken Jeanne so Marianne woke her and brought her to the bedside. Aunt Jeanne was strangely calm, stroking Isabelle's wispy hair and constantly assuring her that the doctor was on his way. Madame Grislot moved about, noiselessly, pressing a milk coffee into their hands and trying to feed warm water to Isabelle in a spouted cup. They all looked up at the doctor's arrival but the careful shake of his head confirmed their fears. As the light grew, Isabelle faded and by the end of the hour, she was gone.

Madame Grislot motioned Fabrice to take both Jeanne and Marianne out of the room. Her Aunt had barely said a word since the doctor's announcement of death and as Marianne steered her from the room a single whimper escaped Jeanne's waxen face.

The doctor gave Jeanne a sedative and advised her to return to bed. Marianne escorted her Aunt to her room and, after seeing the Doctor to the door, she finally had the blessed comfort of Fabrice's arms around her as she gave way to the kind of tears she had not shed since childhood.

John Graves arrived in time for the funeral and these arrangements took over their lives. Relatives from Uncle Grégoire's family needed to be alerted and every resident of the village had appeared at the house to pay their respects, many blessing Isabelle's name as they reported instances of kindness that they had received from her. The funeral itself had lasted almost two hours as these remembrances were repeated from the Church pulpit and the funeral supper had been full of well-wishers who came to offer help to both Jeanne and Marianne.

Uncle Grégoire's family had turned out in force but had been noticeably silent during the funeral and at the supper. Gradually, as the number of villagers and friends dwindled, only the priest, Isabelle's doctor and the Grégoire in-laws remained. This group of relatives had congregated in the dining room and were ranged around the room on the hard-backed chairs that had been drawn back from the refreshments.

John entered the dining room, having seen the priest to the door.

"The Doctor and I are having a glass of warmed wine by the fire in the lounge if you wish to join us" he offered.

Grégoire's nephew, Bernard, got to his feet.

"We will not bother you, tonight," he said, including the various members of his family in his statement. "But we will return at your convenience, tomorrow, to settle the details of the will."

"I am not altogether sure that the will has yet been authenticated by the lawyers," responded John, looking round for the Doctor who had been one of the witnesses

"No, no. I assure you, everything is prepared for tomorrow. I spoke with the probate lawyer, today. He understands our urgency. It makes sense for us to move into Les Jonquilles as soon as possible since our son is getting married in March."

The Doctor had entered the room as Bernard was speaking and John turned to him, astonished. The Doctor responded to John's unspoken enquiry, without acknowledging Bernard's son who had jumped to his feet and was providing blustering and red-faced support for his father's demand:

"My understanding is that the house is passed down the male line. Obviously, Isabelle, as Grégoire's widow, had the right to live here until her death but there were counterclaims at the time of Grégoire's death and now the law will certainly uphold the original codicil."

With a look of triumph, Bernard gathered his family together and, as he turned to leave, could not stop himself from declaiming:

"At last, justice has been done. Sadly, not in my father's lifetime but, at last, our own has been returned to us."

He stared hard at John as if some protest had been made but John's face still showed amazement: not dispute.

The family left the room and John unthinkingly pulled one of the dining chairs towards him.

"Do you think Jeanne knows?" he asked the Doctor.

"In truth, I think Jeanne knows very little. It was always Isabelle who dealt with official matters: Isabelle even seems to have convinced Jeanne that she was 10 years younger than her actual years!"

John slowly shook his head. "So she was actually well into her nineties? That explains some of the reminiscences that I have been hearing from the villagers. Well obviously, Jeanne must be told about the house, immediately, before the reading of the will. Marianne and I have no hesitation in offering her a home with us, in England, but whether she will be prepared to leave France is another matter."

In the event, Tante Jeanne was confounded and dismayed by the news of the house. She alternated between periods of loquacious high spirits when she declared herself well rid of anything to do with Grégoire's family and periods of equally hysterical silence when she rocked gently to herself and wept. She failed to attend the reading of the will and Marianne stayed with her, in her room. John was present and had to suffer the jubilation of Grégoire's relatives as Les Jonquilles was bequeathed to them and then their dismay when they heard that Isabelle's savings were to go to Marianne and that the cottage, at present tenanted by Madame Grislot, had been left to Jeanne, free of any encumbrance. The end of February had been agreed for Jeanne to vacate her home and while John accompanied the lawyer to Paris to investigate Isabelle's bequests, which were mostly tied up in bonds and other investments, Marianne was left to prepare for departure.

Jeanne had absolutely no intention of leaving Saint Gervais and even less intention of turning Madame Grislot out of the cottage. One possible solution to the impasse had been suggested by Madame Grislot herself. She had approached Marianne, with heart-rending shyness, and asked if Jeanne would be prepared to move in with her. Madame Grislot's husband had died some years before and her only daughter had married and moved away. She explained that she was lonely but also afraid that the lawyers might force her from the cottage whether that was Jeanne's wish or not. Gazing at the floor, she had assured Marianne that she would, of course, continue to pay rent. Her one concern was that Jeanne would find the cottage too humble compared with Les Jonquilles.

COMFORT AND A PROMISE

During all the upheaval, Fabrice had kept in the background: acting as messenger when requested and paying anxious attention to Marianne and her Aunt. It was he who was tasked by John to help Jeanne gather her personal possessions together and to help Marianne make an inventory of the contents of the house and stables.

Marianne and he had entered the stables together, discovering an antique pony trap that had obviously not been used in years and equally ancient garden equipment mouldering under a tarpaulin. A pile of musty-smelling sacks lay in the corner and mildewed harness hung from the wall like leafless ivy. Although still January, surprisingly warm sunlight edged its way through the cob-web-curtained windows and turned the dust motes into a sparkling haze. Marianne moved around the dark corners like a wraith: her face pale and pinched from the nights of watching over Jeanne. Tears gathered in her eyes, at the slightest provocation, and she had the air of a convalescent; her usual liveliness cloaked in slow-moving sorrow. Fabrice, gaining permission with a look, wrapped another shawl around Marianne's shoulders. Tilting her head to thank him, in a dream-like movement, she put her hand up to his cheek and then, astonishing herself as much as Fabrice, she kissed him enquiringly on the lips. Fabrice drew her to him with a murmur of delight but, just as quickly, he sprang back and turned as if to leave.

"I thought you . . ." appealed Marianne, her face displaying a gamut of emotions: from shame to anger - and her eyes filling with tears.

"If you only knew!" he exclaimed, pushing her even further away. "This is my greatest wish. But you are in mourning: you need comfort: not passion. I cannot take advantage of you in this way."

"You cannot take advantage but you can refuse me and humiliate me. You cannot take advantage but you can remain in control and tell me what I do and don't want!"

Marianne flung the shawl from her shoulders and it wrapped around her feet as she turned to leave. Grabbing her to steady her, Fabrice stumbled too, grazing her face with his shoulder as he prevented her from falling. Distangling themselves, they both stepped back and eyed each other like foes, wary and at bay. The traces of their breath curled upwards in the crisp mid-morning air and neither of them spoke.

Fabrice slowly opened his arms and his fierce look melted into one of welcome.

"You know that I love you, Marianne. There is nothing more certain. And you know that I want you in every way and that, as soon as this sad time is past, I will ask your father to give us his permission to marry. Don't turn your head away. Come here, please. Let me hold you. Marianne, look at me."

Fabrice moved forward and drew her to him. He kissed the top of her head gently but fervently and cradled her like a troubled child. She spoke into his chest, as if to herself.

"You may indeed love me, but you don't need me. If you did, you would not stop me from loving you." She trembled with the effort of holding back her sobs. "Everyone dies. Everyone dies before they really know how much you love them."

"Come," he said, raising her chin in his hand, "they know, they know." He drew her to him and kissed her with a passion that swathed her in warmth and sent breath-taking tremors through them both. They parted, astonished, with the same soft smile suffusing each of their faces.

"All will be well," he said, releasing her as he heard the carrier's cart making its way round to the back of the house. "Go back in. I need to see that they load Tante Jeanne's things and take them off to Madame Grislot's. She does not want one item of her life here 'picked over' by the heirs. Apparently, they have insisted that their solicitor checks every item of the inventory to ensure that none of Grégoire's belongings leave the house." He turned to go but could not resist one last, brief kiss before releasing her.

John had returned from Paris that evening and, despite being travel-weary, had asked to speak to Marianne and Jeanne straight after supper. The details of the properties would all be settled over the next few weeks but the surprise brought back from Paris was the extent of Marianne's inheritance. Great Aunt Isabelle had made a number of quite small investments into a railway bond that had increased in value dramatically over recent years. The legacy by no means made Marianne into an heiress but the money would certainly buy her a small home of her own in France, for example, if she cashed in the bond.

Marianne's first thought had been to do exactly that so that her Tante Jeanne could benefit from her good fortune but Jeanne was adamant that the move to Madame Grislot's was ideal as long as Marianne still spent time with her and did not get "swallowed up by the English". Since matters were not yet settled, John was to return to Paris the next day and stay until all the papers had been transferred into the correct names. His plan was then to return to England, leaving Marianne to help her Aunt move. The Duke had sent his condolences and had urged John to take as much time as he needed. He had agreed that Monsieur Dupres should stay in St Gervais until the house move was completed and Marianne could return to England.

THE SCANDAL

Lord Wellesden and Lady Frasier's wedding preparations were reaching crisis point and it was still only January. The wedding was to take place at St Paul's, close to the Baron's mansion house which overlooked the Thames and no expense had been spared. March 1st fell on a Thursday and only London friends and close family would attend the formal reception straight after the ceremony. County friends would travel to New Hall for a less formal celebration at the weekend.

Portia's temper had not been improved by the endless round of decisions that needed to be made. She interfered with each of her mother's suggestions while complaining bitterly that there was no one to help her, terrorised the tradesmen who anxiously tried to follow out her commands and only deferred to the Baron's wish that she should "leave it to his very competent staff" when her hysterics threatened to ruffle his equable life-style so that he finally intervened.

Lord Harry Wellesden had grown accustomed to their daily meetings being tense and argumentative and longed to be back in the country. He felt events drawing him further into a drama where he was both a central figure but also, ironically, an outsider. His opinions were not sought: nor did his presence appear to be particularly relished except when he and his fiancée attended some public event at which they received congratulations and good wishes and smiled a lot.

Even so, he was unprepared for the lack of courtesy that

marked his latest visit. He had arrived mid-morning as a misting of rain was finally clearing from the Thames. With very little sleep the night before, and the air in his bachelor flat still heavy with tobacco and port wine, he resented the absurdly early morning call that was delivered to him by his intrepid valet. The first tap at his bedroom door had produced no sound out of his Lordship and a more determined approach had resulted in a flukishly well-aimed boot thudding against the door and the valet deciding to shout the message from the relative safety of the hallway rather than delivering it to Lord Wellesden personally. Portia had stressed the absolute urgency of his getting to her as soon as possible but now that he was seated in the library, with the thin sunshine pulsing in time with his headache, Harry regretted complying with yet another of Portia's demands and wondered that the Baron had also put his name to this particular request.

It was the Baron who came into the room and he looked as out of sorts as Harry when they shook hands.

"Sit down, my Boy. I've ordered coffee; it will arrive shortly. I'm grateful to you for coming so quickly." The Baron took a seat himself and shuffled the pages of a book left open on the escritoire. He pulled on his side whiskers and looked toward the door for the sound of the coffee arriving. The Baron had always treated Harry well – as if he were a junior version of the Baron's own social self: an affable man of the world. But Harry also knew him to be an astute businessman whose fearsome network of well-nurtured contacts belied this easy-going first impression. The Baron's unusual diffidence was therefore disconcerting. Their coffee having been poured and the maid dismissed, the Baron cleared his throat and Harry's anxiety level rose as he thought back over recent escapades that may have come to light.

"You will hear this soon enough so Portia thought it better that you hear it here first. That damn foolish sister of hers has run off with some fly-by-night with no money and even less honour and is nowhere to be found. Her typically nonsensical note declared that she was off to the wilds of Erin to become Mrs James Dehan."

Harry mastered his inclination to smile but could not prevent a gasp of relief and surprise. He quickly turned the surprise to his advantage by shaking his head in disbelief and then springing to his feet. Pacing the length of the library, he fixed a look of offended pride to his face before returning to where the Baron was sitting.

"This is an outrage. The bounder needs horse-whipping. And Sophia! Has she not thought of her family's good name?"

"I feared that you would see it this way, my boy. Portia, I swear to you, is beyond reproach. She knew nothing of the affair and finds her sister's behaviour totally unacceptable."

The Baron moved to stand beside Harry and lowered his voice.

"We are not even sure she has married the fellow. The note was found yesterday evening but she had left the house much earlier, ostensibly to visit a friend. If we could actually find her and they are not yet married, there is still a chance of bringing her back to her senses before her little adventure becomes common knowledge. In the end, that may be our best hope."

Lord Harry refused to meet his gaze and the older man was once more thrown into uncertainty. His portly figure sagged and his jowls trembled as he took Harry by the arm.

"Portia is beside herself. If you will just see her and assure her that you do not regard this absurd situation as any reflection on her and that it has no effect on your intentions with regard to . . her . . . or your future together. . . . . . "

Harry interrupted, with an air of noble condescension:

"Sir, my feelings for your niece remain unchanged. I will need to share the situation with my parents but I too would like the business to be settled as quickly and quietly as possible and I will certainly do what I can to comfort Portia."

"I am proud of you, my Boy. I have always been a man to look after my own and I will not forget your generosity. My niece is desperate to see you and seek your assurances. I will ask her to receive you in her sitting room, shortly." The Baron took Harry's hand.

"Thank you, my Boy."

Alone in the library, Harry let out a hiss of pleasure and punched the air. The moral high ground felt invigorating. The thought of Portia cowed and awaiting his assurances filled him with glee. He stopped in front of the fireplace and preened himself in the ornate mirror that hung above it. "Well now!" he speculated to his reflection, as he raised an amused eyebrow. "Well now!"

AN UNDERSTANDING

February had arrived before John left France. He had met with legal difficulty in Paris and Fabrice had crossed and re-crossed the Channel to provide John with proofs of his marriage certificate and Marianne's birth. While Fabrice was away, Marianne had helped her Aunt sift through her possessions and decide what to take with her. She had also acted as her secretary. Tante Jeanne had commissioned work to be done on the Grislot cottage so that it made a better home for herself and was better able to accommodate visitors. Work would begin in the Spring but the plans needed a thorough eye.

The tension between Marianne and Fabrice during his short, infrequent visits to Les Jonquilles fed on itself each time he left again. Marianne came to resent her Aunt's incessant fussing when he appeared: never leaving them a minute to themselves.

"And here is Marianne when she was first confirmed," she said, passing a photograph to Fabrice whom she had invited to take tea with them. "She looks so like her mother, it is uncanny. Wait, wait, I will show you." Delving into her sewing bag, Jeanne offered a miniature for his inspection. "I found it in dear Isabelle's desk. It must have lain there for years. I don't suppose that even Marianne has ever seen it?"

Fabrice handed the portrait on to Marianne. Painted on porcelain and set in an enamel case, with an intricate gold surround, the miniature was exquisite. Her mother looked to be in her teens, her long dark hair falling down her back in a thick plait entwined with ribbon. Her face was half turned from view but her eyes looked out of the picture with a soft, fresh, openness and her lips curled upwards with the suggestion of a smile.

Marianne was dumbstruck and looked to her Aunt.

"You see, peas in a pod!" her Aunt declared, addressing Fabrice and pointing between the photograph he held and the miniature that Marianne was now refusing to relinquish.

"I have never seen this before," she said, shaking her head sorrowfully. "Did you find other things of hers? My father has so little." Marianne's eyes filled with tears and with a nod towards her Aunt she excused herself and stumbled out of the room.

Annoyed with herself and totally flustered, Tante Jeanne stood up, sat down and then, with apologies to Fabrice and murmured self-recriminations, she turned to the door as if trying to decide whether to go in search of her niece.

"Monsieur Dupres, I think I must say, farewell, for now. I understand you return to Paris this evening by train and, as you can see, I need to go and make amends."

"That had been my intention but they are having problems on the line and it now makes no sense for me to set out before tomorrow. This is my last commission from Mr Graves and then he intends that I give my full effort to helping you with the move."

"In that case, I would be grateful if you could join us for supper. It is only of our own making but far better than you will find at the Auberge in the village."

"That is very kind of you, thank you. I wonder if I might also take up my former quarters in the study, just for one night, if that does not inconvenience you. I have already taken a room at the Auberge for the days leading up to your house move but I was not expecting to need to stay here, today."

Unsure of the etiquette of such a situation, Tante Jeanne protested that of course he must stay but she did not formally offer Fabrice one of the guest-rooms and before she had brought to mind where she might accommodate him with due propriety over the longer term, he had re-stated his intention of staying at the inn on his return from Paris. The temporary accommodation was therefore agreed.

"The eiderdown and pillows are as they were, I believe. Grégoire's study will be our last port of call in rounding up the very last of our family possessions. I will see you later this evening, however? It is the least we can do."

"With pleasure," he replied escorting Jeanne into the hallway. He then scooped up his traveller's valise and headed for the study.

In the event, Fabrice and Jeanne dined alone since Marianne had cried herself into a sick headache and did not come down for supper. The two of them retired early but not until Tante Jeanne had heard some more of le Comte de Gilles and an edited version of Fabrice's childhood. Meantime, Marianne slept fitfully; with haunted dreams in which her mother's image appeared beside her in the school yard and interposed itself in long-gone church outings that her mother could not possibly have attended. The dreams were not frightening: they were disturbing and tantalising and Marianne twitched and fluttered in her sleep. Towards midnight, she woke as if at a call and while she could not remember the dream exactly, she sensed that she had been waving her mother off to an evening event. Her mother had been dressed in white and wore a fine cape but her hair hung down to her shoulders as she would never have worn it in public. Tears started back in her eyes but a look of quiet determination stole over her face as she peeled back the goose-down quilt and stole out of bed.

Fabrice had forsaken the couch and made a nest of cushions and quilts in an alcove to the side of the fireplace. On entering the room, Marianne would not have spotted his improvised bed except he stirred and mumbled in his sleep. Barely breathing, she slid in next to him. She allayed his instant alarm by placing a finger to his lips and nestling closer.

"Do not send me away," she whispered. "I shall love you. I am not afraid. I am more afraid that we will never have a chance to love."

Fabrice held her silken body next to his and kissed her with feverish abandon. Marianne could feel his hardness up against her belly, hampered by his nightshirt. Slowly, she inched her hand under its hem and took him in her trembling fingers, fixing him with a look approaching triumph.

"You see, I am not afraid." She drew her own gown from her shoulders and rolled his shirt up over his waist. Her breath came in tiny pants and her eyes glistened through the darkness. Fabrice moaned, a keening sound as filled with pain as pleasure. He turned his head from her as she nestled into his shoulder and then, answering his body's imperative, he turned back to cup her face, almost roughly, in his outstretched hands. His voice thick with emotion, he whispered endearments into her hair and anointed her eyes with feather-down kisses as he eased his body onto hers.

"My love," he murmured. He slid his hand across her breast and slowly carved a circuitous pathway down into her pubic hair. Now it was she who moaned, eerie cries of surrender that trembled through her limbs, her arching back and soft-hard nipples. Fabrice entered her with care. Marianne let out one short gasp but then pulled him down into her, squirming voluptuously. As he began to move inside her, she stretched out her arms, clawing at the cushions to either side, her eyes preternaturally wide and gazing into nowhere. Fabrice climaxed quickly and with muffled sobs. He rolled back into the cushions, pulling her over with him so that she lay full length, along his body. Neither spoke. Both listened to the beating of each other's hearts, slowly subsiding beneath the sex-flushed skin. Fabrice slowly stroked her tousled hair.

"I did not hurt you? No? Are you sure? I have so little experience. . . . and I had lost all sense."

She placed her finger to his lips and nuzzled into the fine hair in the cleft of his chest.

"Do I look as if you hurt me: or do I look like a woman who has just loved her man and has been loved back in return? If there are things to learn, we will learn them together. You know I am an apt pupil."

She smiled coquettishly and pulled back to sit astride his loins. In the darkened room she could just see the glint of his eyes and the sheen of his shoulders as he reached out to her.

"I must leave at dawn in case my Aunt should hear - but that is hours away." She leaned forward, her hair brushing across his chest as she whispered, "We could do some learning now . . ."

Fabrice pulled her down to him, turning onto his side, one hand encircling her breast, the other bringing her up onto his thighs so that he enclosed her from behind.

"My most beautiful and most well-beloved pupil, first we will lie quietly and I will hold you like this. Then we will have our first lesson. You can teach me and I can teach you" he promised, as she snuggled back into his embrace

They had opened the curtains to get the first stray glimpses of the dawn but lay exhausted as the day crept slowly above the horizon. They had guided one another to their secret places and the reward for their hours of study was a slow build-up of tantalising strokes and kisses that culminated in rampant cries that would have raised the village if Fabrice had not smothered Marianne's mouth with kisses and focussed his own orgasm into a silent scream that left him gasping for breath and glistening with sweat.

As the light grew stronger, they lay in the aftershock, with occasional shudders running through their bodies. Fabrice cradled her in his arms, delicately planting kisses on her neck and shoulders.

"I must go," Marianne muttered, without moving one inch.

"Most sadly, yes, you must. Your family cannot discover our plans in this way . . . I must approach your father. I still feel a sense of shame at taking advantage of you."

Marianne pulled at a lock of his hair. "And you think I would have let you refuse me?" she demanded. "My dear husband-to-be, we are together now, we will be together always. My father will take you as the son he never had and he will know that I am safe and happy in your love. We will tell him as soon as we return to England. A few days and then the world will know and you can woo me as you should."

Fabrice drew her fingers to his lips but continued to look troubled.

"You say he will accept me as a son but will he accept me as the husband of his lovely daughter. I must complete my plans so that he sees that I deserve you. I will take him to the farm that I intend to buy. Just one more big win and I will have enough. I can sell the yearling too."

Marianne raised herself onto her elbow and turned his face towards her as he stared into the middle distance, rehearsing his plans.

"You seem to think I am naïve, but even I know that we cannot live without money. And I have been left some money by Tante Isabelle. I can help you buy the farm and you could keep your lovely yearling – you could name her after me! We can be married straightaway. I have it all worked out." She dwindled to a halt as her words drew no reaction from Fabrice.

He turned to look down at her and scowled as if he had not quite heard what she said.

"You surely don't think that I would use your money?" he asked her softly but with a hint of steel embedded in the tone.

"Our money!" she replied brightly.

He got to his feet, wrapping a quilt around his waist.

"Marianne, don't you see that your inheritance just makes it worse for me. I don't deserve you in my wildest dreams and now this difference in wealth. . ."

Appalled at the effect her news had had, Marianne leapt

up beside him.

"Fabrice, look at me! It's a silly sum of money. It's not as if I am an heiress! I just wanted to show you that I can help you – we can be together that much sooner – we don't need to wait. Don't be angry with me. I can't bear it!"

He wrapped her with him in the quilt and the frown melted from his forehead.

"What am I going to do with you? There is no one I know with half your spirit yet now you are drawn to helpless tears. My brave, soft-hearted girl. I'm not angry with you. I just love you too well and I want you to be proud of me as I am of you." He kissed her face and pulled the quilt more tightly round them both.

"Do not fret. All will be well. I will race Espérance when we get back as well as Folie and when my hurdler wins, his price will rise and I can sell him on, along with the yearling. Don't look like that – I sell them gladly so that we can be together. Just promise me that you will wait until after the race. It is less than a month away and it means I can go to your father with the deeds of the farm in my hand and not be such a beggar for your love."

"Hardly a beggar!" she retorted, once more smiling playfully. "I will wait. I want to wait. I will go with you to my father and he will see I am already yours. He knows how wilful I can be but he also loves me dearly and would wish me to be happy."

As they embraced, both heard a creaking on the stairs as Tante Jeanne came down for breakfast. Marianne stifled her desperate gasp of alarm in the folds of the quilt.

"Thank God she came straight down and didn't call into my room to see that all was well. I'll creep back up there and then wait until she worries when I don't appear. There's more than an ounce of truth if I tell her I've had a disturbed night and decided to sleep in."

"You are more of a minx than I took you for – and so young and innocent at first acquaintance!"

Marianne gave him a playful pinch and tiptoed to the

door. With a glance over her shoulder, she slipped through the doorway and went noiselessly upstairs.

When her worried Aunt appeared at her bedside two hours later, she had slept a blissful sleep. Complaining of a restless night, she managed to express her disappointment at not having said farewell to Monsieur Dupres with the right amount of regret, and no secret smiles. As she bathed and clothed herself, she planned her pattern of behaviour for the next few days. Happily, the bustle of the move would occupy them both. Then the two of them would have the Channel crossing to themselves before their return to the proprieties of New Hall. She gave herself the luxury of conjuring up his face and lingered on the memory of his urgent kisses. Combing her hair back from her face, she pinned it into place and then composed herself before going down to join her Aunt.

A SCANDAL AVERTED

The Baron had asked the Duke of Newshire to meet him at his Club. Although it was barely afternoon, he had fortified himself with a brandy and water and was rehearsing his viewpoint, alone, in a private room. He was settled deep into an enormous leather armchair that creaked in a well-worn, gentlemanly way, as he rose to his feet. Snow-filled rain slashed against the window and the indoor lights had already been lit. The Club had stayed with gaslight and one of them burned unevenly, creating a flicker and a soft, popping sound. The mantle needed changing and the Baron glared at the offending lamp for interrupting his present train of thought.

The Duke was announced and entered the room with an air of decision, quickly dispensing with the formal greetings.

"My grandson has informed me of the situation and your proposed solution. Far too close to rewarding bad behaviour, in my opinion, but I can well see how it came to this."

The Baron urged his guest to take a seat and drew the brandy forward but it was refused.

"It sticks in my gullet just as much as yours. The man's a charlatan. Too much to say for himself and no moral fibre." The Baron struggled for words and grew red in the face.

The Duke took pity on his old friend. "The perfect politician, some would say!" He exchanged a grim smile.

"All may yet be well. My acquaintance with your youngest

niece is only recent but I think she has her husband's measure and will keep him up to the mark, despite her fey manner and her seeming lack of concern for social convention."

"It was she who suggested the plan – although she claims that he has long held political ambitions. Quite how she knew that Drayton was becoming vacant defeats me. Our candidate was well on his way to securing the seat until his father's death decided him against running for election. My sense is that they are both pretty shrewd underneath his charm and her theatricality. I dare say he'll do no worse a job than some others in the House – he has had legal training after all – and this solution at least lends them the air of respectability."

"You are completely certain that they are married? Harry tells me that she makes her views on 'artistic freedom' pretty clear to all and sundry."

"They are indeed married. Married at Gretna Green, like a runaway shop-girl. I'm told they stayed at a local hotel during the 21 days needed to get the licence: signed in as William and Dorothy Wordsworth and spent their days walking among the hills!!! In the meantime, her mother was beside herself and all our investigations – which it's true were centred on Ireland – had been in vain."

"At least it's settled ahead of Harry and Portia's wedding. The Press would have had a field day. I hope Portia and her mother make sure that Mr and Mrs Dehan keep a suitably low profile?"

"It is part of the 'arrangement' that's been agreed with them both: otherwise I think she would have made a spectacle of herself on that occasion too."

The Baron looked down at his hands with palpable embarrassment.

"How is Harry with all this? I understand he'd met young Dehan, socially, a time or two but he could not have welcomed the prospect of this kind of notoriety clouding his wedding day."

"In truth, my grandson has surprised me. The incident seems to have added to his resolve to marry."

As if conjured by the reference to his name, the younger Lord Wellesden was reported to be in the lobby and enquiring whether he might join them. The Baron sent the messenger back to ask Harry to come up and he once again took the Duke by the hand.

"When he sees what I have done for the undeserving Dehan, it is to be hoped he knows that I will do much more for him. My niece has money of her own but, in marrying her, your grandson has more than a dowry. He has as good a friend in me as if I were her father and I will ensure he gets his true deservings."

A MARRIAGE CELEBRATION AND A PROPOSAL

Harry and Portia travelled to New Hall the day after their wedding but preparations for their arrival had been taking place since the beginning of the year. Marianne had only recently returned from France. She had been up to the Hall to offer any help she could give in arranging flowers or place settings but she had not seen the elder Lady Wellesden, who had been much occupied in London. The wedding at St Paul's had been a spectacular affair only mildly affected by an uncommonly fierce storm during which rain had fallen as sleet and careful orchestration of cars and carriages had been required. The news from the London reception had arrived ahead of the couple. The London Pictorial held full accounts of Baron Fraser of Drumdoon escorting his niece to the church and descriptions of the more eminent guests featured on the social pages of all the lesser publications, while even the Times reported the unusual step of the couple taking the title Frasier-Wellesden so that the Frasier name should not disappear for want of a male heir.

The senior staff and the major tenants were invited to the Hall for the evening's festivities. Tables were laid for them in the long gallery and the newly-married couple made an appearance on the "minstrels' balcony" to share a toast and receive congratulations. Marianne was placed between her father and Robert Baker: both of whom vied for her attention. She appeared wan and distracted, however, her thoughts wandering to the less sedate celebrations that would be taking place elsewhere on the Estate in which Fabrice would no doubt be taking part.

Robert escorted Marianne home at John's request and he delivered her indoors before turning to leave.

"I will leave you to your bed. Attending to your Aunt during the sad times in France must have been exhausting?"

"Mr Baker - sorry, 'Robert', as you keep reminding me to call you. What a poor neighbour I am. There's a heavy frost tonight. You must have a hot toddy before setting out for the farm. I know how to make just the thing. Come into the sitting room, it will only take a moment."

When Marianne returned, Robert was still standing and his attempts at helping actually severely hindered her attempts to hand him a steaming tankard of toddy. He finally took the tankard from her, but then placed it back down on the tray, pulled at his jacket tails and heaved a bewildered sigh. Meantime Marianne moved over to the rocking chair alongside the sofa and was surprised to find Robert standing over her when she had settled herself. He sat in the corner of the sofa so that their knees were almost touching and then, realising their proximity, he hutched himself further away. Marianne looked into his guileless face, as he began to speak and then fell silent. They then both spoke at once and she insisted that he begin but, once again inspecting his coat tails, he begged her to go first.

"I was merely going to remark that marriage seems to suit Lord Wellesden . . . . He seemed elated when they appeared on the balcony."

"Yes, I think all men need marriage at some point," replied Robert as if they had been debating the subject long and hard and this was his ultimate conclusion.

"Ahh, but do all women?" retorted Marianne playfully, trying to open up the conversation that had run aground on Robert's sententious tone.

Seizing his chance, Robert moved back closer to her and finally looked her in the face.

"It is not all women that I want to know about, Marianne. It is only you. What are your feelings about marriage?"

Robert's look was so tortured that for one beat of her heart Marianne thought that he had by some means found out about her relationship with Fabrice and blushed to the roots of her hair. Her silence and obvious confusion seemed to give Robert heart and he slid from the sofa onto one knee.

"Will you marry me?" he asked, stressing the me as if he were the end of a very long list.

Instinctively, Marianne tried to make him rise and they both bobbed and curtsied, almost knocking heads in some awful comic dance. Finally, Marianne motioned him to sit back down and then stood herself.

"Robert, I had no idea. I have known you since I was a girl and you know how much I like and respect you – how I have always liked and respected you."

After looking up at her with eyes full of love and hope, Robert looked down at his hands.

"It is not that I don't care for you," she said, making matters worse. "I … you need to understand that I am not… ."

Before the words "free to marry" had left her lips, irrevocably, Robert had stood to his feet and was trying to make his farewells. He made a move toward the door. Picked the tankard up and put it down again, looking anywhere except at Marianne.

"There is no need, my dear girl. No need. I should have guessed as much. No, no – please let me see myself out. Really, really. I think I knew in my heart of hearts. Please don't leave the fireside. Your father will be back shortly, I know. No hard feelings, my dear. All forgotten, all forgotten. We will still and will always be the best of friends."

As soon as Robert left, Marianne rushed around the sitting room putting out the lights. Breathlessly, she removed all traces of his visit. Leaving a light in the hallway, she whisked off to bed before her father could return, anxious to avoid enquiring looks or even perfectly innocent conversation about the night's events.

THE STABLES

The cold spell at the beginning of March continued. Jem had wrapped his hands in sacking to wheel stale bedding out from the stables to the newly opened heap behind the barn. Even so, the cold seared through the metal handles of the barrow and he stopped halfway to blow on his reddened hands, totally regretting having left his gloves on the dresser at home. The cobbles rang with the sound of his boots and the pock-marked pathway to the muck-heap rasped like slate as the barrow jigged and bobbed over the ruts and crannies. Nolly was supervising the tipping of the new loads, which were being placed in a fenced-off area to the left of the well-rotted manure. His wispy white hair escaped from an enormous scarf that had been tied and retied round his head and neck and tucked into the belt of his overcoat at the back. He wore matching fingerless gloves and brown leather gaiters that half-covered his boots and wrapped round the bottoms of his corduroy trousers. Jem smiled to himself as he imagined the fuss that Nolly had put up before his granddaughter had sweet-talked him into wearing Marianne's hand-knitted gifts and sent him out to work swaddled up against the cold like a wizened schoolboy. The stable lads knew full well where to put the new-made muck but none of them cheeked the old man as he pointed out the misty pile and made them pick up any bedding that had fallen off the overladen barrows.

Jem parked his empty barrow next to Nolly. He had

grown even taller since the summer and his thin neck angled out of his jacket as unprotected as a baby bird. Now that he stood still, the blood came back into his hands and a grape-red glow ran up over the aching wrists that his last year's jacket failed to cover. He fumbled in his leather waistcoat.

"I was told to bring you this," he explained, offering Nolly a lint-bound flask.

Nolly reached out with a gnarled hand.

"She's a good girl, that one. Tha's brung it, so it's ony fair tha'll 'ev some wi' me?"

Jem swallowed, in anticipation, and his Adam's apple bobbed in his throat. Steam rose up from the flask as Nolly poured its contents into tin mugs that he pulled from the gaping pockets of his overcoat.

"Aye, broth!" he said. "There's nowt like it. And tha'll not taste a better drop than thissen."

The two of them looked back beyond the stable yard at a group of riders setting off down the drive, their outlines picked out in silhouette as a thin sun lit up the landscape.

"I see the Frenchie's won again, then? He wor racing down in the next County and he beat all on 'em!"

Jem radiated borrowed glory.

"You should have seen him! He took him over the sticks as if the horse was born to it. Made it look easy. Raced him with the Duke's blessing so he says although it's more like his Lordship's blessing since he made a fair bit out of the betting. His Lordship may even buy the horse now Mr Dupres's so set on selling. Just when he's got him going well. It makes no sense to me."

"Don't tha be so sure – buying a hopeless 'carriage' horse for tuppence and selling

t' same animal as a champion hurdler for a king's ransom - it makes a good deal of sense to me. These Frenchies are cleverer than they look!"

"And there's the very man," said Jem, pointing back over to the stables. "I think he's helping Miss Marianne with Sage this morning once he's exercised Hidalgo."

"I imagine he is," replied Nolly. The suggestion of a wink formed in his rheumy eye. "Tha's best go and see if tha's needed too. It's thee that's kept that pony in such fine fettle while she's been away in France."

Jem watched as Marianne put Sage through her paces. Despite not having ridden for several months, she rode with expert ease gaining delighted praise from Fabrice who had her turning perfect circles at either end of the school. He was teaching the pony to get down on one knee so that Marianne could mount, without a block, whether she was wearing breeches or not. Horse and rider had just succeeded in this manoeuvre when applause rang out from the far side of the ménage. Sophia stepped forward, followed by her husband, both of them flushed from their ride in the brisk morning air.

"My 'Master of the Horse' will have you in a circus yet, Miss Marianne. The spangles and feathers would suit her, would they not, James?" James Dehan stepped into the ménage alongside his wife and looked down at his feet as Marianne brought Sage round to them.

"I believe you have already met Mr Dehan, Miss Marianne? Or the Right Honourable Member for Drayton as he now is." Sophia managed to announce James' title with a hint of sarcasm at the same time as fixing Marianne with a look of triumph.

James stepped forward with an outstretched hand.

"We are old friends," he smiled, looking not at Marianne but at Fabrice who had joined them. "Or rather we are old friends by virtue of Miss Marianne's long-time friendship with my brother's wife." He turned to offer his hand to Fabrice before continuing:

"I understand Anne and my brother intend returning to her parents' house for the last two months before the happy arrival. My poor sister-in-law has not been at all well." Sophia grimaced as James shed a look of concern around the group. "I imagine she could be back in Newshire before the end of the month if matters do not improve."

Lord Frasier-Wellesden arrived ahead of his wife. Portia's face was thunderous with irritation and she twitched her riding crop against her side as she tried to keep up with him.

"There you are!" he declared, in general greeting, but with his eye fixed on Fabrice.

"I had been looking for you, in particular, Mr Dupres. I understand Espérance is kept elsewhere?"

Fabrice stepped forward and gave a suggestion of a bow to his Lordship and a more courteous recognition to his wife.

"I had hoped to see the animal later this morning - Put him through his paces, that sort of thing."

Portia let out a sigh of exasperation. "I have no intention of scampering around the country just to get a glimpse of some horse or another," she declared.

"I have no intention that you should either," her husband responded. "I would wish you to accompany your sister and Mr Dehan back to the Hall. I have no need of your company, on this occasion."

Sophia turned to see if Portia would take up the challenge. Lord Frasier-Wellesden's tone had been civil but determined and Portia was unused to being told to stay at home. Sophia saw her sister bridle and then think better of responding. She watched Portia's colour rise as she affected an air of unconcern and contrived to look bored. A power shift was taking place that filled Sophia with amusement. She wondered if her sister secretly preferred some aspects of her newly-stern husband.

THE EXPLANATION

The weather having picked up, John Graves readily agreed to Marianne visiting the Bakers – and even stood by his word when she expressed her determination to ride there on horseback. Robert's farm was barely two miles distant and John had ensured that Robert would be looking out for her so it was with a mixture of pride and trepidation that he saw her off.

The farmhouse stood in the crease of a hill, its mellowed local stone in sharp contrast to the brash modernity of recently-added barns and outbuildings, built to accommodate Robert's increasing dairy herd. Robert came to the door himself and revealed the table already laid out for their lunch. His housekeeper had "done them proud", as he had declared. Robert seemed in holiday mood: his work clothes having been put aside for a dark tweed suit that matched his station in life and yet looked oddly out of kilter with his burly frame and diffident air.

"I'm glad you came to visit," he began, having checked Marianne's every need, several times, before finally settling her at the table.

"I was worried after the last time we met."

Robert rubbed his hand through his thinning, greased-down hair, leaving it spiked out on top and sticking to the folds of his neck, behind; emphasising the disparity between his stolid suit and his general agitation.

Marianne smiled warmly.

"That's just it. I owe you an explanation," she said, noticing the colour that welled up into his weather-worn face as their eyes met. "An explanation from the other day - when we spoke of marriage."

Robert fidgeted with his cutlery and cleared his throat. A barely conscious possibility of hope formed in his chest and suppressed his ability to speak.

Quickly, Marianne continued:

"I need to explain to you why I could not marry you – cannot marry you – But I will need your promise to respect my confidence for a short while."

Robert nodded his consent, the colour once more rising to his face.

"I cannot marry you because I am engaged to another – or rather, I have promised to marry someone else."

Robert raised his head, interrogatively, but still remained silent.

"I know my father would be shocked and dismayed – not at my choice – but at the secrecy that has been necessary." Marianne leaned forward and continued earnestly.

"But my husband-to-be is a good man; and, most importantly of all, I love him."

There was a long pause; accentuated by the ticking of the oak-cased clock on the mantle-shelf.

"I don't know what to say," Robert finally mustered.

"I think that is one of the reasons that I felt able to tell you," Marianne replied tenderly, placing her hand on his arm. "That, and my wish to let you know that I had not taken your proposal lightly – that I have every respect for it: and for you."

"Right – well - I can't say that I'm not disappointed – I am. And I can't say that I'm not concerned about your father not being a party to this arrangement. But I have respect for you too, Marianne. Enough respect to believe that you know what you are doing."

Marianne gave him a radiant smile.

"I knew you would understand and I knew I could trust

you. Thank you, Robert."

Relieved, Marianne finally took in her surroundings and the small banquet of food in front of her.

"Let's eat!" she declared. "Let's eat and talk of other things or we'll give offence and that would never do."

They did eat and they did talk of other things, albeit in a desultory fashion. But Robert's nervousness continued and it was not until after he fetched Sage round to the front door, and Marianne was on the verge of leaving, that he took her hand, under cover of helping her to mount.

"I need to give you an explanation too, Marianne. You see, I knew that you weren't interested in me as a husband – Why should you be? I'll not see forty again. I'm closer in age to your father than I am to yourself - But I've always loved you since you were a little girl. And that day I saw you with my sisters' children, it made me think how good a mother you would be . . . . it made me choose to ignore our differences . ." Robert sighed and looked away, letting go of Marianne's hand. "I've been a fool."

"No, no. Not a fool. You just wanted what we all want. Love, a family . . . . and the woman that can give them to you will not think you or herself foolish. She will have found a good man, Robert."

Leaning down from the saddle, Marianne kissed Robert on the cheek and asked the patient Sage to walk on. Robert watched until she disappeared from view and then walked slowly off toward the barn. The housekeeper drew back from the window, disappointed. She had viewed Marianne's lingering departure from a very different perspective and was hoping that congratulations were in order but she knew that Mr Baker kept his own counsel. His face never gave much away, and when he re-entered the house, he neither looked jubilant nor dismayed.

THE FINAL RACE

The race meeting known as "the Prems" was held on the last Saturday of March and was always well attended. Horse-fanciers had given it the nickname since many of them regarded this meeting as the preliminary to the traditional flat season, the first meeting of which took place at Lincoln, in April. Lord Frasier-Wellesden was attending the event as his final engagement before leaving on honeymoon and his mother had decided to join the party. Her husband had needed to return to Germany on business and activity helped soften the effect of his absence. Marianne more than gladly agreed to accompany her. Few others from the Estate were able to travel to watch the race but Jem had been given time off to act as groom to Folie.

The effects of an overnight frost had soon burnt away under the force of a surprisingly strong sun that glanced off the newly-painted stands and sparkled in the grass. Some of the cars and carriages had their hoods down and the ladies' light-coloured costumes heralded the springtime even though the wearers had taken the precaution of fur stoles and muffs. Lady Wellesden had forced a fur wrap onto Marianne, eliciting a look of annoyance from Portia. Her daughter-in-law's temper had already been roused by Lord Frasier-Wellesden disappearing from her side as soon as they arrived at the Course and not long after, Portia excused herself to join some friends who were inspecting the runners in the Ring.

Marianne settled the rugs around Lady Wellesden and attempted to describe the scene to her as a means of masking her own excitement. Fabrice was in the first race – a two mile handicap that meant three circuits of the track. A win, today, would leave them free to approach her father. Marianne was tired of the subterfuge. Over the last month she had become quite wan-looking and her lack of spirits communicated themselves to Lady Wellesden, despite Marianne's attempts to seem at ease.

"This is the first time we have had a chance to talk since you returned from France. My son's wedding and Lord Wellesden's business in Europe have preoccupied me. I have missed you, Marianne."

Marianne took Lady Wellesden's hand.

"And what of you, my dear? You are your usual attentive self but you too seem preoccupied, troubled .."

Marianne blushed and looked down.

"Foolish of me," continued Lady Wellesden. "I am forgetting your recent bereavement and the responsibility that you had to take onto your youthful shoulders?"

Evading the implied question, Marianne twisted round in her seat and remarked that the riders seemed to be leaving the Ring. The chauffeur had drawn the car to the side of the track, back from the finishing post so as to avoid the crowd in the Stand but their party was well-positioned to see the whole circuit since the trees that would normally have obscured the Start had still to gain their full leaf.

The riders came on to the track, their colours interweaving in graceful-seeming waves as they vied for position; the actual tension of the Start diluted by distance. For Fabrice and Folie, in the centre of the riders, the semblance of grace was imbued with jittering menace and Folie tossed her head and whinnied, distressed by the jostling of the other horses.

The crack of the starting pistol drew all eyes to the Start and, as the tide of horses turned and streamed down the track towards them, Lord Frasier-Wellesden unexpectedly re-joined them. He had removed his greatcoat and was looking hot and flushed despite the fresh breeze.

"Would you not prefer to be at the Finish?" asked his mother. "Marianne and I can manage perfectly well."

"Sorry?" he replied, evidently not having heard. In his agitation, he pulled at the side of his beard, gazing back along the Course, his eyes never leaving the oncoming riders.

His mother shook her head and exchanged a smile with Marianne.

"Men and their hobbies! This outing has taken precedence over every preparation for the honeymoon."

The horses galloped past as they came near to the end of their first circuit and Marianne half jumped to her feet as she spotted Fabrice in the colours of the French flag. He was toward the back of the first group that was led by a lithe-looking grey whose rider sported vivid purple. The leading horse was holding close in to the rails and setting a very fast pace. Where the sun had softened the ground, saps of mud squirled off the horses' hooves as they turned the bend and headed away.

"I asked the chauffeur to place a bet on Monsieur Dupres," admitted Lady Wellesden conspiratorially. "We have to back the home side, I think?" Her last remark was aimed at her son who had swung round to keep the riders in view as they began the second circuit.

"I'm afraid to say that the home side is not really cutting it at the moment - Although Folie was showing as favourite around the Course earlier today," her son added, his face was set in a concentrated frown and he was still fretting with his beard.

The horses were returning to the last bend before the finishing straight; their heavy breath providing counterpoint to the sound of their hooves as they passed by. Bystanders started moving toward the Finish-line to be ready for the final circuit and Lady Wellesden wondered at her son's not joining them. Their chauffeur was obviously experiencing torments at having to stay with the ladies and gave a loud halloo as Fabrice moved up the leading group and brought Folie alongside the grey. Lord Wellesden stood resting his hand on the windshield. He gasped and clenched his fist round the frame as the grey fell back and Folie took the lead ahead of an earlier back-marker.

Shouts drifted back from the Stand as the riders started on their final circuit. The chauffeur lost all decorum and was bellowing for Folie and Lady Wellesden gripped Marianne's hand as she assured her that Folie was still ahead. With her Ladyship's encouragement, she too stood up beside Lord Wellesden as the horses came back into full view for the final time.

Folie and a last-minute entry, Emerald, were now well out in front; the grey having completely faded. Sweat ran down their flanks and foamed in the creases of their necks; their riders poised forward as if in prayer. As they turned the bend and made for the Finish, Marianne could just make out Folie through the tail-enders as the little mare clung to the rail, neck to neck with Emerald. But, in a heart-stopping moment, Marianne's shout of encouragement turned to a frantic, ghoulish scream as, with a spasm that almost threw her from the car, the name, "Fabrice!" burst from her lips. Turning his back on the mayhem that was unfolding on the track, the chauffeur barred her way as she scrambled to get out of the car. With immense presence of mind, he lunged forward and caught her, successfully stopping her fall as she fainted back down into the seat.

Lady Wellesden moved to Marianne's side while the chauffeur and Lord Frasier-Wellesden rushed onto the track. The scene before them was transformed into Armageddon. Tail-runners swerved and barged each other in a desperate attempt to avoid collision with the pitiful Folie who had crashed through the inside rail and was impaled by a stake. The badly-wounded mare was lying on her side, squealing, as Emerald raced, oblivious, to the Finish. A dappled horse had also fallen but she got tentatively to her feet as onlookers dashed to the riders' aid.

Fabrice lay partly underneath his mount, her blood seeping into the gaily-coloured silk of his shirt. One arm was splayed out in front of him; the other was bent back under his body, entangled with a cross-piece from the rail. As Folie trembled and groaned beside him, he lay completely inert. A stretcher team was running back down the track and several riders had reined in and were milling about in front of the Stand, still some yards from the Finishing post.

The Clerk of the Course arrived with the vet. Fabrice had been pulled out from underneath the still squealing Folie and was being rolled onto a stretcher. Raising her head Folie sighed and turned her eyes to the vet, letting out one last, shuddering whinny as he quickly put her out of her misery. Stable lads were running onto the track to take charge of the horses that were still at the scene; their riders dismounting to speak with the officials.

Lord Frasier-Wellesden stood back from the group crowding round the Clerk of the Course and barely seemed to realise that the chauffeur was addressing him.

"Your Lordship, excuse me, your Lordship – but shouldn't we go and tell the Clerk about what we saw. He might need witnesses. It was quite obviously the Irish fellow's fault. Folie was leading until Emerald's rider slashed her in the face with his whip. I saw it as clear as day. He did it twice and Folie careered off the track when Monsieur Dupres tried to check her."

Lord Frasier-Wellesden stepped in front of the chauffeur, menace and fear combining to turn his face into a grotesque mask.

"Stay where you are, man! There is no need for you to be rushing forward telling the Clerk his business. You are needed back at the car. How could you leave her Ladyship and Miss Graves? Go back immediately. I will deal with this."

"But did you have as clear a view as me, your Lordship? Won't the Clerk need all the information he can get?"

"I am sure the Clerk has all the information he desires.

There is a mass of people clamouring for his attention."

"But were they standing right on the corner as we were?"

"Well, there's the thing. I was standing with as good a view as you and I saw no whip; no interference whatsoever on the part of Emerald's jockey, in fact. You must have been mistaken."

"But – your Lordship!"

"Just go back to the car! If you must make these accusations, write them down and I will ensure that they are delivered to the Clerk as soon as possible. In the meantime, our duty is to the Ladies. Go back and help my mother with Miss Graves. I will find my wife and join you immediately. Well, don't just stand there, go on, man!"

NO HOPE

Fabrice had been moved to the Cottage Hospital not far from the Estate and a surprising number of the Estate staff had been to visit him. Faced with his inert form, many had gradually shuffled off, embarrassed and unsure how to behave, but Jem and Nolly still took turns in sitting with him every day and telling him their news.

His surgeon had seen service with the military and compared Fabrice's state to that of those who returned from war. It was he who had operated on the crushed arm, finally taking the decision to remove it from the elbow down but managing to save Fabrice's left leg where the fractured bone had come out through the thigh. Softly spoken and with an unassuming manner, he had endeared himself to Marianne who also sat beside Fabrice on a daily basis and chatted to him, as the doctor advised. She was mostly accompanied on her visits by Amy, for propriety's sake, but Lady Wellesden also took her in her carriage and was growing increasingly concerned about her.

Two weeks had passed and, on this occasion, Lady Wellesden had stepped out of the room to speak to the doctor and left Marianne reading a letter from Tante Jeanne to the ever-silent Fabrice. At one point, he stirred and Marianne leaned forward with a sharp intake of breath, but he had merely suffered a spasm of pain; there was no hint of consciousness. The other beds in the small side ward were empty: their occupants having recovered and gone back to their lives. As the cloud thickened outside, the beds gleamed in the dim light of the ward and an unearthly quiet reigned. Marianne rested her hand on Fabrice's hollowed cheek and her gaze willed him to wake until Lady Wellesden's echoing footsteps signalled her approach and sent Marianne hastily back into her seat. The doctor had escorted Lady Wellesden back to the Ward but having checked the charts, he withdrew and left them alone.

"I need to speak with you, my dear. May I sit with you? There will be no more visitors today and the doctor has asked me to share his concerns with you."

"Concerns?" responded Marianne. Lady Wellesden winced at her own ineptitude.

"The doctor has said nothing to me about concerns!" Marianne continued. "Fabrice is certainly no worse! He moved today – just now, while I was here; he stirred and seemed on the verge of speaking."

"It's true, he is no worse. They are managing to keep him on a liquid diet and his wounds are healing well. In truth, the doctor's concern is with you, Marianne. He sees you here every day. He sees the unwavering hope and belief in your eyes . ."

"And what? Am I not supposed to hope: not supposed to believe? It's only two weeks: the doctor himself told me about cases where patients had been in this state for months and yet they still recovered."

"I know - I was there. But he also told us about those who never regain consciousness or whose bodies finally release them from this half-life by closing down the functions needed to support them."

Lady Wellesden moved closer to Marianne. Her companion's beautiful young face was contorted in silent sobs and her shoulders shuddered with the effort of containing her tears. Lady Wellesden just as silently wiped her own eyes.

"The doctor still has some hope but as the days go by his hope lessens. It may be weeks before they know the outcome . ."

"It can be weeks – years, as far as I'm concerned. I will wait."

Lady Wellesden drew Marianne towards her as the younger woman glared with fierce determination at the recumbent figure in the bed.

"You have time - but what about the baby?" she whispered.

Marianne started and let out the suggestion of a whimper. She leaned into Lady Wellesden's shoulder.

"There is a baby, isn't there?" asked the older woman, gently.

Marianne sighed and lifted her head. With the same fierce pride with which she had declared her determination to wait for Fabrice, she looked Lady Wellesden in the eye and answered yes.

"And, of course, it is his: Monsieur Dupres, Fabrice. The child is his and he is mine. We planned to marry as soon as the race was won and he could buy the fields he's been renting. Fabrice didn't think my father would accept him as a son-in-law until he could see that he was able to provide for me."

Marianne grimaced to stop the tears from falling.

"And it's all a nonsense. I don't need providing for. Thanks to my great-aunt, I have money of my own. It's a nonsense. A cruel, wicked nonsense. And the irony is that I now have a child who has no father and the shame of that fact will kill my own father and leave me completely alone."

Refusing the comfort of Lady Wellesden's outstretched arms, Marianne rocked in the chair, cradling herself; keening with grief and self-pity.

"Mine was a guess but I am certain that your father knows nothing. He almost raised the question with me, in his careful way, as to why you were visiting here with quite such regularity. He sees your concern for the young man as part and parcel of you suffering the trauma of your great-aunt's death and then witnessing the accident at the racecourse. I think your father has immense compassion beneath that proper exterior. Are you sure you shouldn't tell him? It won't be too long before the whole world will start to guess."

In her discomfort, Marianne got to her feet and was readying herself to leave. With an air of brisk efficiency she delivered what seemed like a rehearsed response.

"I have a while before I need to worry on that score and by then, Fabrice will be well. We will marry here, for my father's sake, and we will live in France, so that the baby's date of birth will be shrouded by distance and the wagging tongues will have to do their sums. No-one need ever know: we will be together and my father will be saved from disgrace."

Lady Wellesden shook her head as Marianne struggled to sound convinced.

Marianne sank back into the chair and cried into her hands.

"But what else can I do? I can't leave here while he is still like this – Otherwise, I would have left for France already. I need a father for my baby – Fabrice can't die: he must wake up. . . He can't leave me. I can't do this on my own! And I can't make my father pay for my mistake."

With a look of sudden defiance, she sat back upright.

"But it's not a mistake!" she declared. "How could it be a mistake? – Our baby is not a mistake – it's not a mistake, it's not a mistake!"

Forsaking the pretence of control, Marianne tore at her hair and sobbed hysterically. Lady Wellesden finally captured her and drew her into her arms. Frantic sobs came out of a body that hung as limp and uncomprehending as the figure in the bed. Marianne's hands dropped to her side and she gave herself over to her grief.

"I want to die," she murmured, almost interrogatively, raising her face to Lady Wellesden.

"No, no, don't say such a thing. There has to be an answer. There will be an answer. But the doctor does not think that answer will be Monsieur Dupres regaining consciousness within the next few days . . . . . The message I was asked to deliver is that Monsieur Dupres' condition is exceedingly grave. You need to take into consideration that he may well die."

Lady Wellesden strengthened her grip on Marianne as she squirmed in protest at her comforter's harsh statement, squinting her eyes in an attempt at denial.

"I know you must hate me for repeating what the doctor said. But he has been telling you himself and you seem not to have heard. . . Believe me Marianne, I would give anything to see Monsieur Dupres completely well and the two of you happy. Why would I not want everything you want for yourself? You know how dear you are to me."

In the face of Marianne's despair, Lady Wellesden's own attempts at staying brave dissolved. The two of them clung to each other as day darkened and the white of the hospital beds glimmered in the dusk. A nurse looked in at one point, intending to light the lamps, but she did not disturb them and when she next looked, they had gone.

THE CHURCHYARD

Crows and magpies cackled and croaked in the top branches of the oaks: the outlines of their nests just visible through the stark newly-sprouted leaves. There were also signs of life among the ancient yews that bordered the churchyard as the busy feathered homebuilders set to work, preparing for their offspring, swooping down with their lopsided loads. A cold wind blew from the East and the tops of the trees bowed forward under its force like old men trudging up a road, denying the quickening signs of life among the cavorting daffodils and day-old blossom.

A scattering of carriages was drawn up behind the church and the rumble of the organ escaped through the lead-bound windows; their lush stained-glass drained of colour by the frost-pinched skies. Birdsong took over once again as the service in the church quietened into the hush of contemplative prayer and the far-off siren of a steam train wafted in on the wind.

A respectably-sized congregation stood to its feet as the vicar gave the final blessing and the organ notes pierced the chill of the day to herald their departure. Friends greeted one another in hushed voices as they moved into line; families jostling to be together. As the vicar moved into position, the organist opened up the stops and notes cascaded among the buttresses, alarming one tired toddler to the point of tears and his parents to embarrassed laughter and comforting hugs. The intricately carved west doors were heaved back from the hewn-stone archway of the porch and a bleak Spring day edged into the nave.

Both bride and groom started as the bells rang out: the groom breaking into a smile as his bride gripped his arm to begin their progress down the aisle. Breaking with tradition, Marianne had replaced her veil and it trailed down over her shoulders, mingling with the satin folds of her dress and obscuring her bouquet. Robert Baker angled his arm so that she had his full support and solemnly acknowledged the congratulations of those still standing in the pews.

Remarks had been made about the suddenness of the announcement and Robert's sisters regretted the lack of bridesmaids but comforted themselves with the thought that their children would have been in stunned awe of Lady Wellesden, who acted as Matron of Honour. Their outfits easily outshone the rest of the ladies since Marianne's friend, Anne, was not able to attend; her baby being due in a month. Marianne joined them in expressing disappointment but intimated, as did her father, that the marriage had been spoken about, among themselves, for some time and Robert's housekeeper gained status locally from her claim that she had known about it for a month or more.

Bride and groom stopped in the lea of the doorway as the photographer arranged the shot and Robert discreetly lifted his wife's veil to reveal her to the world. As pale as the blossom woven in her hair, Marianne looked up into his eyes and smiled her gratitude. Her father moved to her side as Robert squeezed her arm. The greetings of the congregation were added to the sound of the bells as the wind buffeted round the side of the church, ruffling the finery of those intent on throwing petals. The bridal carriage was brought round, bells jingling on the harness and the seat banked with flowers. Bride and groom were leaving directly for the station, the illness of Marianne's Aunt being the reason given for Jeanne's non-attendance at the ceremony and for the couple's wish to be in France as soon as possible. Mr Graves was hosting a lunch for his fellow farmers and had promised a more general celebration when the married pair returned home. There were tears in his eyes as he saw them both off in the carriage and the congregation dispersed.

As if called by the bells, a smaller cart appeared at the far side of the churchyard, edged in behind an ivy-covered wall. Nolly was at the reins with Jem beside him and lying along the length of the cart was a muffled figure, desperately straining to look out over the top of the weathered boards. Jem jumped down from the seat and squatted behind the swaddled shoulders to provide a backrest.

"Can tha just see the tops of their 'eads?" Nolly asked, urging Jem to cover the figure back over with the blankets that swathed him from head to toe.

"That doctor's going to 'ave me put in the 'ospital when he finds out what we've done! He said it ud kill you to move: never mind roaming round countryside in a cart."

Fabrice attempted a smile: his brackish skin was stretched across his skull, his nose was etched into prominence and his hair crept out, faded and wispy, from the blanket wrapped around his face.

"I will not tell, if you will not, as you English say. In fact, my good friends, you must not tell! No one must know that I have 'returned from the dead' as the admirable Doctor put it. We have kept the miracle quiet for one day, we can keep it quiet for one day more if you will help me." A shadow crossed Fabrice's face and his jaw slackened as if on the verge of sleep. Jem pulled the blankets up closer and signalled to Nolly to get underway. Rallying himself, Fabrice turned to the boy: "Or, as our old friend says, the cart ride will be the end of me and then the problem is solved."

Once again Fabrice moved back to the boundary of consciousness and when the cart went over a rut the only sound from the slouched bundle was a stifled groan. Nolly and Jem exchanged a look.

"I don't know what's 'urt 'im most," said Nolly, his gnarled hands tensed around the reins.

"I do," replied Jem. "I wish I hadn't told him but it was

the first thing he asked about. I almost fell off the chair when he just came out with it. There I'd been, talking to myself for a month and then he asks for Marianne as clear as day – just as if he'd been having a lie-down for a minute." Jem looked at his knees with a hangdog expression and picked at the seat-board with his fingernail. He looked towards Nolly.

"What else could I have said? I told him that she'd been there every day but not that day because she was getting married the day after. He would have found out from someone if not from me, wouldn't he? I didn't think before I said. I just thought . . ."

"There's no use blamin' tha sen, Jem. It's 'appened and the less Miss Marianne knows the better."

Jem glanced behind to check on their passenger as they started up the drive to the hospital. Fabrice was sleeping but tears were settling in the pockets of his eyes and the sight of the broken man's sorrow forced the boy to turn away.

EPILOGUE

WAR IN FRANCE

Saint Gervais was a long way from the Front but the War was becoming increasingly real. As the German troops moved with terrifying speed across Belgium and, as skirmishes across the French border began, some local farmers had taken to hiding their horses and their winter stores.

Marianne had arrived in the early Spring of 1914, having been contacted by Madame Grislot who feared that Tante Jeanne did not have long to live. In the event, her Aunt rallied and Marianne's role as nurse provided her with blessed activity as she came to terms with widowhood.

Robert's death, nearly two years ago, had caused significant changes. Robert had left the farm to Marianne and John had stepped back from full-time management of the New Hall Estate to supervise Newbold farm for his daughter. Robert's elder sister and her husband now farmed much of the land that Marianne had gifted them after Robert's death (land which she had bought from the Estate after her marriage) and she had made a handsome gift of money to the younger sister to enable her and her husband to move to Canada. In that sense, Marianne had only inherited much of what she already owned but this concerned her much less than causing the kind of ill-feeling that had arisen over Uncle Gregoire's property in France.

At the same time, with the Duke becoming increasingly frail, his son, Viscount Wellesden, had returned home and was developing plans for the Estate. The Viscount had appointed a young Deputy Estates Manager to support John. He had settled in well and there was every reason to think that he would take over full management, eventually.

In St Gervais, the warmth of March had finally tempted Tante Jeanne out into the garden. Swathed in blankets, with a tasselled hat perched on her head, she looked almost as small as her great-niece, Annette. Happily, they also shared the same spirit and their dark sparkling eyes mirrored each other's as Marianne's daughter insisted on pushing "Grantie Jeanne's" wheelchair onto the patio.

"She is so like your mother," smiled Jeanne. "a complete urchin, yet she still spends time with her bedridden old Aunt. Look at her now, all tender concern as she carries the kitten back to its mother. 'Attention, ma Cherie'," she cried as she saw Annette hopscotching around the little pond. Annette blew kisses and moved marginally away from the water as Marianne smiled and shook her head.

"She is a complete daredevil but has Robert's common sense, thank Heavens. He could not have been a better father to her. He loved me with a generosity that I could never repay but he loved Annette, intuitively, unthinkingly. He was there at her birth. She rode on his shoulders as a baby and then trailed around after him every day of their lives together. I loved him but she adored him."

Marianne was quick to pick up on her Great Aunt's quizzical look. "Of course I loved him. Who could not love him? Such kindness – and then, towards the end, such bravery. He was a good man . . . ."

Marianne moved forward to tuck the blankets around Tante Jeanne's knees.

"I don't think I ever told you how our 'arranged marriage' came about? I had told Robert that I loved another when I refused his first proposal. It was only after Fabrice's accident and my much- remarked-upon visits to the hospital that he came to realise who I had been speaking of when I told him that I was engaged to marry someone else.

I was in despair. No one expected Fabrice to live. My father was concerned and confused by my behaviour; only Lady Wellesden knew that I was pregnant. Robert would not have known had he not sought me out at the hospital one day and treated me with such gentle respect – while re-stating his love and support for me - that I confessed to him that Fabrice's death would dash my hopes and plans in more ways than he could have imagined.

His very next thought was to 'save' me and thereby protect my father from the repercussions of my shame. He quietly and calmly persuaded me. He made no demands. It was an agreement between friends: one of whom had a seemingly unsolvable problem. It was sealed with a handshake: not a kiss. I had been back out to Newbold and had once again come under scrutiny from his housekeeper who managed to interrupt our meeting numerous times with concerns about the quantity of cake or hot water. John's final words as I left still haunt me. He held onto my hand as he helped me into my little pony cart. 'Thank you,' I said. 'You are a good and kind man.' and he replied, in his bluff way: 'Nonsense, you are a good and honest woman'. And, of course, that is what he enabled me to be, in the eyes of the world, an 'honest woman'."

"Maman! Maman! We have a visitor," cried Annette as she spied someone in a tall black hat approaching the gateway set into the hedge that surrounded the garden. She ran to her mother and whispered, in English, "It's that funny man again". Marianne frowned a reproach until she realised that Jeanne's face showed as few signs of welcome as her daughter. "Ahh, Bernard," she murmured, with something approaching a sigh. She moved forward to take his hand and the normally ebullient Annette moved into the shelter of her mother's skirts.

"Madame Baker, Chere Jeanne," he said, removing his hat.

"Tante Jeanne has just been enjoying her first trip into the open air . . ."

"Yes, indeed," agreed Jeanne "but I have begun to feel quite chill so I am afraid you must excuse me." She looked meaningfully at Marianne who narrowed her eyes in her Jeanne's direction.

"I will help you, if I may?" offered Bernard.

"Really, there is no need. My daughter takes pleasure in helping me push 'le chariot' as she calls it."

"Ahh, the little Mademoiselle. Bonjour ma petite." Annette moved even further behind her mother and ignored his outstretched hand. Prodded by her mother, she looked up at him.

"Good morning, Distant Cousin," she said, in English. "It is such a pity that I need to go indoors with Grantie Jeanne . . .", and with a hint of a handshake she turned her attention to the "chariot".

"Still, she fails to understand French? Such a pity since we all hope that she may come to call France her home."

Marianne motioned for Bernard to be seated while she took Jeanne indoors and ordered refreshments. All three sets of sparkling brown eyes exchanged an amused glance. Annette was, in fact, truly bi-lingual. So much so that you could ask her something in French and she might well reply in English – or vice versa. It seemed to depend on which language she was thinking in at the time or whose company she was in. However, she always spoke English to Bernard and always addressed him as Distant Cousin as if this were his name. It was her way of keeping the "funny man" at bay.

NOT SO FUNNY MAN

As soon as the coffee had been served and Madame Grislot had returned to the house, Bernard got straight to the point.

"As you can imagine, my dear, I am here on behalf of my heartbroken son." His face radiated sorrow and he glanced at Marianne to gauge her reaction. Her face remained impassive. "You can't fail to accept the ardour of his affection when you look back over the months that he has been offering you his hand in marriage." Bernard reached forward to take her hand but Marianne busied herself with her coffee cup. "And then, of course, there is the joy that it would bring to the whole family and the very great benefit that uniting your fortunes would bring to you both. The inheritance from his dear departed grandmother and his own undoubted abilities have made him a rich man – but a lonely man. He had to forsake much to follow his fortune during those years in Paris. . . ."

"Yes, I did hear that his intended marriage never took place. Yet I thought there had been an agreement from his youth?" Marianne put the question forward with the air of a card player who knows she holds an ace. It certainly disconcerted Bernard. He crossed and re-crossed his legs and cleared his throat noisily.

"Ahh, yes. The follies of youth. Happily he realised very quickly that the girl was not for him – too young, a country girl, poor as a church mouse once one looked into things. How could she possibly sit alongside a man making his way in the world? No, no, not suitable at all. I assure you that he has put such folly behind him. He now truly appreciates your worth as a future wife and has asked me to assure you that, as your husband, he will offer you his devoted protection and accept Annette as one of his own."

Marianne smiled, but not at the thought of the delightful prospect that was being presented to her. She was remembering the various encounters between Annette and Bernard's son and the rather scandalous word that Annette had recently used to describe him – a word that she must have heard from the mouth of a workman or passer-by. Even at their first meeting, Annette had cowered before him like a frightened pup and then kicked him soundly on his shins: totally unexpected behaviour that earned her an early bath and no supper.

Finally, Marianne sat forward. "I am very pleased to have had this chance to clearly understand each other. Whilst being aware of the honour that your son has extended to me, I can only repeat and this, for the final time, that I have no intention of marrying him. My firm intention is to return to England as soon as Jeanne re-gains her strength. My father misses me and needs me and he and I can provide a much more secure future for Annette and, indeed, Jeanne - in England."

Bernard's face became transfigured. A white spot appeared in the centre of the deepening red of his cheeks and his mouth twisted into a snarl as he tried to interrupt, but Marianne continued: "Please thank your son for me but please also inform him that any further advances will be regarded as an impertinent intrusion and that he will not be welcomed into this house."

Bernard stood, as if to strike her or shake her into submission. He stuttered profanities and his eyes stood out from his head. Unintimidated but determined, Marianne stood, turned her back on him and returned to the house.

REVELATIONS

It was not until Annette was in bed that Marianne and her Aunt managed to talk. Jeanne had dozed for most of the afternoon but, after a light supper, she seemed to revive.

"Eugh, that man – I don't know which is worse; him or his puffed up son! It's all about money," she said, with a knowing twist of the head. She smiled at Marianne and blew a kiss: "Not that your personal attractions don't warrant the attention of any man – indeed, far better men than he. Sadly, it has become almost a matter of pride with Bernard. His son is to marry 'the English Heiress'. He has been telling the whole neighbourhood for months now. He barely gave a decent time for mourning."

Marianne shuddered involuntarily. "I know, I hear the whispers as I pass by. How could anyone who knows me think that I would make such a choice?"

"Certainly, those who know you were shocked and concerned – especially poor Monsieur Dupres."

There was an eternity of a second before Marianne blushed and asked: "Monsieur Dupres?"

"Well, yes, the poor man came to present his compliments and to see if I needed any help. Bernard made sure that he was told about your informal 'engagement' in no uncertain terms." Tante Jeanne pulled her shawl more closely round her shoulders and her eyes drooped.

"When was this?" Marianne asked, rather more loudly than she intended.

Jeanne re-focused. "Hmm, not long after dear Robert's death – maybe eighteen months ago?"

"So Monsieur Dupres knows that I am a widow? And he has known this for some while?" Jeanne tried to rouse herself as she noted Marianne's piercing expression. "What did he say? Where has he been? Did he ask about me?" She looked Jeanne fiercely in the eye. "You didn't say anything about Annette?"

"Of course not, that is not my secret to tell – although he must surely have wondered even before he left England and before you had returned from your extended 'honeymoon'?"

Marianne got to her feet, fidgeted with her hair, sighed and paced to and fro but even in her agitated state she noticed that Jeanne had sunk down into the chair and that her face was taking on the weight of sleep. She bent towards her tenderly. "Why didn't you tell me before?" she whispered to herself. Softly, she went in search of Madame Grislot to help her get Jeanne into bed.

THE RETURN

Fabrice was travelling North on a circuitous route that brought him back into contact with some whom he called friends and some whom the world called gipsies. Since his return to France, he had discovered that not all gipsies were thieves and not all thieves were gipsies. Indeed, when he was first well enough to travel, he experienced great acts of kindness from unexpected quarters and some huge disappointments at the hands of those whom he thought he could trust.

His way back to full physical health had been long and his return to riding had involved a specially extended rein that he could rope round his arm just below the elbow. He still suffered mentally. He had conquered the need for alcohol to quieten his nights and his abject self-pity. He had learned to avoid low company once he realised that such companions left him more miserable than before. He had built a reputation for the healing of horses and even acted as midwife to a runaway girl who had joined the ranks of the wandering band who went from village to village helping with the harvest. He had taken bullets out of dogs that had been worrying sheep and sewn up the heads and limbs of men who had survived a brawl. He had studied herbal remedies and learned how to become "invisible" if there was trouble. He had nowhere to return to, so he had made no plans to return. And then, on his way to the gipsy festival at Sainte Marie de la Mer, he heard news of le Comte de Gilles.

Still a young man, le Comte had begun to crumble both in body and mind. Most of the servants had left – some removing valuables in lieu of wages. The land was left unworked and the horses were in the care of a near-blind old man and a youth from the village. The Brothers had helped in the nursing of le Comte but they had their own duties to attend to.

Fabrice's shock on first seeing le Comte was profound. The formerly elegant man was wrapped in a tattered shawl and his hair was matted with food and what looked like down or feathers. Le Comte was equally surprised on seeing him and demanded to know who he was while calling ineffectively for servants to bring his gun. It was only the intervention of one of the Brothers who had been nursing le Comte that prevented further bouts of hysterical aggression. Fabrice was patient but insistent. Gradually, le Comte allowed Fabrice to help him wash and shave. He plaited le Comte's straggly hair with its knitted clumps and bald patches. He made broths so that even with so few remaining teeth, le Comte could eat sustaining food.

And then, one late morning when Fabrice entered le Comte's rooms to draw the curtains, le Comte opened his eyes and, with a gargoyle's smile, exclaimed: What the Deuce: it's the gipsy!!

Fabrice bent over his hand:

"At last you know me? Yes, the gipsy youth has returned as a much altered man. Did you forget my time in your stables and my trip to England to deliver Hidalgo? We have both lived a life since then and it shows on both our faces."

Le Comte motioned to Fabrice to sit him up against the pillows. Fabrice baulked at the paper thin crepe of his flesh and the smell of urine seeping from the covers. The effort of sitting seemed to exhaust le Comte and his eyes stared unseeing at the windows. Fabrice waited.

Le Comte finally said: "Hidalgo? Yes, yes, I have been wondering about my horses. Where are they? Why do they keep them from me?"

Fabrice adjusted the pillows as le Comte's body slowly drooped forward. "They are here, Monsieur le Comte. Not Hidalgo, but many others. That is why I am here. I know how much they mean to you. I have found a good man to help me. I will get them back to fitness. And when you regain your fitness, we can go and inspect them together."

"Another gipsy is it? There will be no horses left to inspect, however fit I get." Le Comte's attempt at a jibe set him coughing and he pointed at the flask of brandy to help clear his throat. "So it looks like you are here to stay then?" Suddenly a look of panic swept across le Comte's face. "You are here, aren't you?" he said, clutching at Fabrice's arm. "You are here to stay?"

"Yes," Fabrice replied. "I am here for as long as you or the horses need me."

In the event, le Comte and the horses needed him for many more months. Fabrice turned the stables into his stronghold and no one dared interfere with him or the horses in his charge. Towards the end, Fabrice would carry le Comte into the stables to view the once-emaciated animals that now gleamed with health and strength. It was le Comte's one remaining pleasure. Even so, when le Comte's will was read and Fabrice learned that he had been gifted the horses, he was taken by surprise. So were le Comte's other beneficiaries, some of whom threatened court action. But the distant relatives who had suddenly appeared had to content themselves with the chateau and its lands and accept that the stables and adjoining fields, as well as the gardens surrounding the Friary; which had been willed to the Brothers, were no longer part of the domain.

On the night of his death, as le Comte sank into a stupor, Fabrice had helped nurse him and listened to his ravings on the subject of Love: - Love the best of all virtues and the worst of all vices. Love as the reason le Comte had no children and never could have. The Brothers understood these tormented ramblings as a sign of religious conversion but Fabrice understood his words differently.

THE REUNION

Annette had been set the task of finding the first rose of summer by her wily mother so that Jeanne could have a quiet nap, but after a few minutes she came running back across the garden, demanding her mother's attention:

"Maman! Maman! There's a man at the gate with a pony. Shall I let him in?" Marianne pulled the excited child towards her and looked at her sternly. "Annette, how many times have I told you not to speak to strangers? The gate is kept closed for good reason."

"But he is not a stranger. He is a pony-man. He says he has brought a pony for Grantie Jeanne. A lovely, lovely pony . ." Annette jumped from foot to foot and tried to pull away.

"Very well, very well, I'll come and see but Grantie has said nothing to me about a pony."

As mother and child approached the gate, the pony-man was bending to untangle the bright red leading rein and tie the pony to a branch. As he turned, Marianne stopped dead and almost fell. The startled child looked up at her mother; but the man had already stepped through the gate, without any invitation, and, with just the slightest encouragement from Marianne, he had clasped her in his arms.

Marianne could now not stop smiling and pulled her daughter forwards with an attempt at introductions. She was making no sense and waving her arms in a dazed way. But, eventually, she roused herself to quickly explain that the pony-man was, in fact, a dear friend of herself and Grantie

Jeanne and that he had often helped Grantie in the past when her family were back in England. "Yes," added Fabrice, "I did not know you were here. I was worried that Grantie might need my help; and the help of a well-behaved pony."

"He said 'Grantie'," chortled Annette, beaming at Fabrice. "Can we wake her, Maman? Can we show Grantie her pony?" Marianne had regained her composure and her wits. "That's a really good idea. Run to the house and find Madame Grislot, please. Ask her to help you, but be gentle – don't alarm poor Grantie."

Annette ran off making so much noise that Grantie would certainly not need to be woken and Marianne turned to Fabrice. They gazed at each other, unspeaking. Now it was his face that was drained of colour. He turned to watch Annette disappear into the house, still shouting for Madame Grislot to "come quick"!

"She is your daughter?" he asked as his eyes welled with tears. "No," she replied: "she is our daughter."

******

Neither Marianne nor Fabrice had any clear memory of how they got through the afternoon. Offers of refreshment and bringing the pony into the garden to crop the grass had eased their way but time passed in a haze of emotion. Marianne marvelled when Annette let Fabrice put her on the back of the pony and hold her in place. Her daughter seemed undisturbed by his injured hand but was intrigued enough to ask him if it hurt. In fact, her questions had come thick and fast and would normally have warranted a reprimand. "Could he speak English? Where did he find the pony? What was the pony's name? Could they call her Mignonne since she was such a lovely pony? When would he drive her in the pony cart?" At one point, Fabrice pulled his hat down over his ears and pretended to be deaf. As a child, Annette might be forgiven, but Jeanne was almost as rude, bombarding him with questions and greeting his replies with a coquettish turn of her head and knowing looks at Marianne.

Even as Marianne put Annette to bed, her daughter was still full of questions. "What had happened to the poor pony man's hand? What was his real name? Where would the pony stay? Would they come back tomorrow?" Marianne stroked her hair and softly sang the lullaby her own mother used to sing. Memories of her first meeting with Fabrice at New Hall floated around her and she placed a soft kiss on her daughter's lips, which were the image of her father's.

Fabrice was staying at the local inn which had also stabled the pony. He ate with Marianne and Jeanne but he did not leave when Jeanne went up to bed and Madame Grislot bade them goodnight. They sat in silence for a while. Fabrice stretched his legs and brushed against her foot but they made no eye contact. Finally, Marianne turned to him.

"You did not come even though you heard that Robert had died?"

"Is that a question or a complaint?" he asked. "I'd come many times before, when passing through, and I always gathered news of you through Jeanne whilst swearing her to secrecy. Then the last time I came, I was told that you were about to marry your cousin and I really didn't want to witness yet another of your marriages." Marianne threw him a mock-offended glance and swallowed a smile.

"And then no more passing through?"

"No, no more passing through. Fixed to the spot by my duty to le Comte. He needed my help and so did the horses. I still can't believe that he bequeathed them to me. In a strange way, he and the Brothers were the closest thing I had to a family."

"Not anymore," she said and moved to sit beside him.

AN UNDERSTANDING

The War had become a reality. St Gervais experienced a flurry of pride tinged with anxiety as young men answered the Call. England had entered the War and bombs had been dropped on Paris. Fabrice had returned to his horses and "hidden" them. He was adamant that they should have no part in a war that was already taking innocent human lives in a cause that, to his mind, was based on jingoism and greed.

Marianne had been under increasing pressure to return to England. Her father had travelled to France in early summer to escort them back but he was forced to recognise that Jeanne was too weak to travel and that the family were as safe in France as England for the time being.

Fabrice and Marianne had been extremely discreet during his visits and Annette had learned to call him Monsieur Dupres, at first, and then Cherami (dear friend) which she pronounced as one word: a form of address which seemed to delight them both. Fabrice had intimated that his August visit would be the last for a while and Marianne had begun to wonder what he was planning. She found out as they walked in the water meadows, close to the house.

"I have saved my horses but I do not intend to save myself," he began, refusing to meet her eye. "I think this War has nothing to do with the likes of me – but France is under threat and although no-one would want me as a soldier" and he glanced at his injured arm, "they will accept me to help with the wounded or keep supply lines open. I am good at helping sick horses and sick men."

"And are you good at dodging bullets?" she rasped as she turned to confront him. "I suppose you think they will not shoot at volunteers! France may need you but Annette and I need you more. You cannot put yourself in danger while we sit and wait for news," she cried, as anger fought with tears.

Fabrice pulled her to him and she gave way to tears as he comforted her. "They say it will be over by Christmas. Half the Princes are related to each other and the Generals all went to the same school." Marianne struck him gently on the shoulder as he smiled at his own exaggeration.

"But what about our plans? What about my father? I am committed to France for as long as Jeanne needs me but . . ."

"We have faced worse separations. If you need to return to England, I will make sure that you are escorted there. The gipsies have little allegiance to France and they have the knack of being invisible and travelling unseen tracks." He broke out into a smile of triumph. "In fact, that may be the very best service I can give to France, using my contacts to move around, invisibly." He realised that his attempts at diverting her had gone too far and drawing her to him gravely said: "The important thing is that we have an understanding. We can now be man and wife, till death do us part, and I swear on my soul that we will grow very old together. We will have a simple ceremony before I travel North and then, whether we are in England or in France, you will be my legal wife as well as the wife of my heart."

"If only it were that easy," Marianne sighed. How could I ever return to England with the very man who had already brought my reputation into doubt?

"The world has a short memory, my love. I will return to England with wealth of my own and, I hope, with the blessing of your father. Furthermore, the world is changing, Marianne. It is changing as we speak. When we return to England together, I think there may be many more widows and many more children whose parentage is suspect. The whole of Europe will never be the same again."

SUMMONED BY BELLS

The land around St Gervais was beckoning to autumn. Crops were already being gathered in and a late August heat-haze rested high above the Church. The leaves barely rustled: even the hum of insects was subdued. St Gervais Church no longer tolled the hour or announced an occasion but a sparkling jingle accompanied the sound of an approaching horse and alerted those waiting in the churchyard. A smart little pony cart with a harness dressed in flowers and bells appeared in the distance. Marianne was driving, with Annette beside her, and she brought Mignonne to a smooth standstill. In front of the entrance porch.

John stepped forward to take charge leaving Madame Grislot to attend to Tante Jeanne as the wedding party filed into the Church ahead of them. As Marianne entered the Church, the small congregation – from which Bernard was noticeably absent – turned to watch her progress. Both bride and bridesmaid were dressed in the palest pink and both carried a posy of country flowers. They were followed by a trail of sunlight, gentle smiles and whispered compliments. Fabrice was the last to turn. He fixed them with a sombre look that he had donned to hide his feeling of utter joy, which would otherwise have overflowed into tears and cries of jubilation. His "old friend" from St Gilles acted as Best Man. Tall and fair-skinned with blond tips to the curls of his long dark hair, Fabrice had introduced him as a trusted acquaintance of le Comte and the stir that such an introduction created seemed to close down further questions; in spite of the flutter that his presence excited among the female members of the congregation.

John was to stay at Tante Jeanne's while Marianne and Fabrice went on a very short honeymoon and the Best Man had assured him that he would, personally, escort him back to the coast. Few people realised just how few non-essential crossings would be undertaken after the Christmas "cease-fire" had come and gone.

The Reception centred on the house but made use of the neighbour's field that was accessed from the garden and was now the home of Mignonne. More guests had joined them and the night was magical: the stars shyly making their entrance into a lustrous dark blue sky.

Having put Annette to bed and embraced Tante Jeanne, the couple left their guests to their brandy or hot chocolate and quietly walked off into their future: a future with little certainty but a future full of hope.

Printed in Great Britain
by Amazon